William Shakespeare, Charles Praetorius, Frederick J. Furnivall

The Troublesome Raigne of John, King of England

the first quarto, 1591, which Shakspere rewrote - about 1595

William Shakespeare, Charles Praetorius, Frederick J. Furnivall

The Troublesome Raigne of John, King of England
the first quarto, 1591, which Shakspere rewrote - about 1595

ISBN/EAN: 9783337388225

Printed in Europe, USA, Canada, Australia, Japan

Cover: Foto ©Andreas Hilbeck / pixelio.de

More available books at **www.hansebooks.com**

THE TROUBLESOME RAIGNE

OF

JOHN, KING OF ENGLAND.

THE FIRST QUARTO,
1591,

WHICH SHAKSPERE REWROTE (ABOUT 1595) AS HIS
"LIFE AND DEATH OF KING JOHN."

PART II.

A FACSIMILE, BY PHOTOLITHOGRAPHY, FROM THE UNIQUE ORIGINAL IN
THE CAPELL COLLECTION AT TRINITY COLLEGE, CAMBRIDGE,

BY

CHARLES PRAETORIUS.

WITH FOREWORDS BY F. J. FURNIVALL, M.A., PH.D.

LONDON:
PRODUCED BY C. PRAETORIUS, 14 CLAREVILLE GROVE,
HEREFORD SQUARE, S.W.
1888.

43 SHAKSPERE QUARTO FACSIMILES,

WITH INTRODUCTIONS, LINE-NUMBERS, &c., BY SHAKSPERE SCHOLARS,

ISSUED UNDER THE SUPERINTENDENCE OF DR. F. J. FURNIVALL.

1. *Those by W. Griggs.*

No.
1. Hamlet. 1603. Q1.
2. Hamlet. 1604. Q2.
3. Midsummer Night's Dream. 1600. Q1. (Fisher.)
4. Midsummer Night's Dream. 1600. Q2. Roberts.
5. Loves Laber's Lost. 1598. Q1.
6. Merry Wives. 1602. Q1.
7. Merchant of Venice. 1600. Q1. (Roberts.)

No.
8. Henry IV. 1st Part. 1598. Q1.
9. Henry IV. 2nd Part. 1600. Q1.
10. Passionate Pilgrim. 1599. Q1.
11. Richard III. 1597. Q1.
12. Venus and Adonis. 1593. Q1.
13. Troilus and Cressida. 1609. Q1.
17. Richard II. 1597. Q1. Duke of Devon-shire's copy. (*Best version; text printed.*)

2. *Those by C. Praetorius.*

14. Much Ado About Nothing. 1600. Q1.
15. Taming of a Shrew. 1594. Q1.
16. Merchant of Venice. 1600. Q2. (Heyes.)
18. Richard II. 1597. Q1. Mr. Huth's copy.
19. Richard II. 1608. Q3.
20. Richard II. 1634. Q5.
21. Pericles. 1609. Q1.
22. Pericles. 1609. Q2.
23. The Whole Contention. 1619. Q3. Part I. (for 2 Henry VI.).
24. The Whole Contention. 1619. Q3. Part II. for 3 Henry VI.
25. Romeo and Juliet. 1597. Q1.
26. Romeo and Juliet. 1599. Q2.
27. Henry V. 1600. Q1.
28. Henry V. 1608. Q2.
29. Titus Andronicus. 1600. Q1.
30. Sonnets and Lover's Complaint. 1609. Q1.

31. Othello. 1622. Q1.
32. Othello. 1630. Q2.
33. King Lear. 1608. Q1. (N. Butter, *Pide Bull.*)
34. King Lear. 1608. Q2. (N. Butter.)
35. Rape of Lucrece. 1594. Q1.
36. Romeo and Juliet. Undated. Q4.
37. Contention. 1594. Q1. (For 2 Henry VI.)
38. True Tragedy. 1595. Q1. (For 3 Henry VI.)
39. The Famous Victories of Henry V. 1598. Q1.
40. The Troublesome Raigne of King John. Part I. 1591. Q1.
41. The Troublesome Raigne of King John. Part II. 1591. Q1.
42. Richard III. 1602. Q3.
43. Richard III. 1622. Q6. (*on stone.*)

TROUBLESOME RAIGNE, PART II.
FOREWORDS.

THIS *Troublesome Raigne* was Shakspere's material for his *King John,* and in the Forewords to Part I, Mr. Rose showd how skilfully (in the main) our Poet used that material, though he faild to make of it a good acting play. With the help of my friend Mr. W. G. Stone, I propose now to give what was probably the old Playwright's material, those parts of Holinshed's and Hall's *Chronicles* (*Holinshed,* ed. 2, 1586-7, vol. iii.) which he used, with a few words linking them together.

The old Playwright starts his first Part with the death of John's elder brother, Richard, 'Victorious scourge of Infidels,' the Lion-Heart of England, and with the sorrow of the land in consequence. On this, and the quality which may have led to the insertion of the Lady Falconbridge incident, Holinshed says :—

(156. i. 46) 'At length king Richard [I] by force of sicknesse (increased with anguish of his incurable wound) departed this life, on the tuesdaie before Palmesundaie, being the ninth of Aprill, and the xj. day after he was hurt, in the yeare after the birth of our Sauior 1199. in the 44 yeare of his age, and after he had reigned nine yeares, nine moneths, and od daies : he left no issue behind him.

A.D. 1199.

King Richard departed this life.

His stature & shape of bodie.

He was tall of stature, and well proportioned, faire and comelie of face . . . .

His disposition of mind.

'As he was comelie of personage, so was he of stomach more courngious and fierce, so that not without cause, he obteined the surname of *Cueur de lion*, that is to saie, The lions hart. Moreouer, he was courteous to his souldiers, and towards his freends and strangers that resorted vnto him verie liberall . . . . .

The vices that were in King Richard.

[Col. 2] 'He was noted of the common people to be partlie subiect vnto pride, which surelie for the most part foloweth stoutnesse of mind : of incontinencie, to the which his youth might happilie be somewhat bent; and of couetousnesse . . . On a time whiles he soiourned in France about his warres . . there came vnto him a

Fulco a priest.

French priest whose name was Fulco, who required the K[ing] in any wise to put from him three abhominable daughters which he had . . . "for thou hast three daughters, one of them is called pride, the second couetousnesse, and the third lecherie "' . . .

Next succeeds King John, the 'second hope' of Queen Elinor's womb (Sc. i. l. 6); and at once the strife between him (then in France) and Arthur begins (*Hol.* iii., p. 157, col. 1) :—

Anno Reg. 1.

'This man, so soone as his brother Richard was deceassed, sent Hubert archbishop of Canturburie, and

Rog. Houed.

William Marshall earle of Striguill (otherwise called Chepstow) into England, both to proclaime him king, and also to see his peace kept, togither with Geffrey Fitz Peter

Matth. Paris. Chinon.

lord cheefe iustice, and diuerse other barons of the realme, whilest he himselfe went to Chinon where his brothers treasure laie, which was foorthwith deliuered vnto him by

Robert de Turnham.

Robert de Turncham : and therewithall the castell of Chinon and Sawmer and diuerse other places, which were in the custodie of the foresaid Robert.

[Angiers given up to Arthur.]

'But Thomas de Furnes, nephue to the said Robert de Turncham, deliuered the citie and castell of Angiers vnto Arthur duke of Britaine. For by generall consent of the nobles and peeres of the countries of Aniou, Maine, and Touraine, Arthur was receiued as the liege and souereigne lord of the same countries.

'For euen at this present, and so soone as it was knowne that king Richard was deceased, diuerse cities and townes on that side of the sea belonging to the said Richard whilest he liued, fell at ods among themselues, some of

[Arthur preferd by some to John.]

them indeuouring to preferre king Iohn, other labouring rather to be vnder the gouernance of Arthur duke of

Britaine, considering that he seemed by most right to be
their cheefe lord, forsomuch as he was sonne to Geffrey,
elder brother to Iohn.   And thus began the broile in
those quarters, whereof in processe of time insued great
inconuenience, and finallie the death of the said Arthur,
as shall be shewed hereafter.'

But Queen Eleanor 'being bent to prefer hir sonne
Iohn, left no stone vnturned to establish him in the
throne, comparing oftentimes the difference of gouernement betweene a king that is a man, and a king that is
but a child.   For as Iohn was 32 yeares old, so Arthur
duke of Britaine was but a babe to speake of.   In the
end, winning all the nobilitie wholie vnto hir will, and
seeing the coast to be cleare on euerie side, without any
doubt of tempestuous weather likelie to arise, she signified
the whole matter vnto K. John, who forthwith framed
all his indeuours to the accomplishment of his businesse.

'Surelie queene Elianor the kings mother, was sore
against his nephue Arthur, rather mooued thereto by enuie
conceiued against his mother, than vpon any iust occasion
giuen in the behalfe of the child, for that she saw, if he
were king, how his mother Constance would looke to
beere most rule within the realme of England, till hir
sonne should come to lawfull age, to gouerne of himselfe.
. . . 'When this dooing of the queene was signified vnto
the said Constance, she, doubting the suertie[1] of hir sonne,
committed him to the trust of the French king, who receiuing him into his tuition, promised[2] to defend him from
all his enimies, and foorthwith furnished the holds in
Britaine with French souldiers.   Queene Elianor being
aduertised hereof, stood in doubt by and by of his countrie
of Guien, and therefore with all possible speed passed
ouer the sea, and came to hir sonne Iohn into Normandie,
and shortlie after they went foorth togither into the
countrie of Maine, and there tooke both the citie and
castell of Mauns, throwing downe the wals and turrets
therof, with all the fortifications and stone-houses in and
about the same, and kept the citizens as prisoners, bicause
they had aided Arthur against his vncle Iohn.'

After Easter, king John was invested duke of Normandy, and
leaving his mother to defend Guienne, he past over into England,
landing at Shoreham on May 25, 1199.

'On the next day, being Ascension eeue, he came to
London, there to receiue the crowne.'

[margin notes:]
A.D. 1199.
[Q. Eleanor

[wins over
the nobles.]

Queene
Elianors
enuie against
Arthur.

Constance
dutchesse
of Britaine.

[Arthur en-
trusted to
K. Philip II.]

Queene
Elianor
passeth into
Normandie.

The city of
Mauns
taken.
Matth.
Paris.
R. Houed.

K. John
cometh ouer
into Eng-
land.

[footnotes:]
[1] safely   [2] p. 158, col. 2.

John's coronation took place on May 27, 1199. During his absence (*Holinshed's Chronicle*, vol. iii. p. 160/1)

N. Triuet.
The French K. invadeth Normandie.
A.D. 1199.

'in England, Philip K. of France hauing leuied an armie, brake into Normandie, and tooke the citie of Eureux, the towne of Arques, and diuerse other places from the English. And passing from thence into Maine, he recouered that countrie lately before through feare alienated. In an other part, an armie of Britains with great diligence wan the townes of Gorney, Buteuant and Gensolin, and following the victorie, tooke the citie of Angiers, which king Iohn had woon from duke Arthur, in the last yeare passed. These things being signified to king Iohn, he thought to make prouision for the recouerie of his losses there, with all speed possible.'

[Angiers taken from John.]

Nearly a year elapst between John's negotiations with Philip II. in 1199, and those which ended in the marriage of Lewes and Blanche (*Hol.* iii. 160/2).

Rog. Houed.
Arthur duke of Britaine made knight.
A.D. 1199.
[Aug. 16]

'About the same time, king Philip made Arthur duke of Britaine knight, and receiued of him his homage for Aniou, Poictiers, Maine, Touraine, and Britaine. Also somewhat before the time that the truce should expire; to wit, on the morrow after the feast of the Assumption of our ladie, and also the day next following, the two kings talked by commissioners, in a place betwixt the townes of Buteuant and Gulcton. Within three daies after, they came togither personallie, and communed at full of the variance depending betweene them. But the French king shewed himselfe stiffe and hard in this treatie, demanding the whole countrie of Veulquessine to be restored vnto him, as that which had beene granted by Geffrey earle of Aniou, the father of king Henrie the second, vnto Lewes le Grosse, to haue his aid then against king Stephan. Moreouer, he demanded, that Poictiers, Aniou, Maine, and Touraine, should be deliuered and wholie resigned vnto Arthur duke of Britaine.[1]

The French kings demand.

'But these, & diuerse other requests which he made, king Iohn would not in any wise grant vnto, and so they departed without conclusion of any agreement. . . . shortlie after a peace was concluded betwixt king Iohn and his nephue duke Arthur, though the same serued but to small purpose.

[John refuses it.]

A peace betwixt king Iohn & his nephue.

. . . 'vpon some mistrust and suspicion gathered in the obseruation of the couenants on K. Iohns behalfe, both

The mistrust that duke Arthur had in his vncle king Iohn.

[1] The Playwright in Part I, sc. iv, lines 160-1, makes Philip II. demand these (with Veulquessine) for his own son Lewes, on his marriage with Blanche.

the said Arthur, with his mother Constance, the said
vicount of Tours, and diuerse other, fled awaie secretlie
from the king, and got them to the citie of Angiers, where
the mother of the said Arthur refusing hir former husband
the earle of Chester, married hir selfe to the lord Guie [Constance
de Tours, brother to the said vicount, by the popes marries Lord
dispensation.' . Tours.]

Sc. i, lines 75-304, p. 7-13, the incident of the brothers Falconbridge and their Mother, may have been adapted in part from the
following story of the Duke of Orleans's bastard son (the 'Bastard of
Orleans' of 1 *Henry VI.* I. ii. 46, &c.) told by Hall in his *Chronicle*,
ed. 1809, p. 144-5, under 'The .VI. year of Kyng Henry the .VI.,'
1 Sept. 1427-8 :—

"Here must I a litle digresse, and declare to you,
what was this bastard of Orleance, which was not onely [The Bast-
now capitain of the citee [Orleans, then besieged by the ard of
English[1]], but also after, by Charles the sixt made erle of
Dunoys, and in great authoritie in Fraunce, and extreme
enemie to the Englishe nacion, as by this story you shall
apparauntly perceiue, of whose line and stemc dyscend
the Dukes of Longuile and the Marques of Rutylon.

"Lewes, Duke of Orleance,—murthered in Paris by
Iohn, duke of Burgoyne, as you before haue harde,—was
owner of the Castle of Coucy, on the Frontiers of Fraunce
toward Arthoys, wherof he made Constable, the lord of
Cauny, a man not so wise as his wife was faire ; and yet [had a beau-
she was not so faire, but she was as well beloued of the Lady Cauny,
Duke of Orleance, as of her husband. Betwene the duke lovd by the
and her husbande (I cannot tell who was father) she con- Orleans.
ceiued a child, and brought furthe a pretye boye called She bare a
Ihon ; whiche chyld beyng of the age of one yere, the soon died.
duke disceased ; and not long after, the mother and the
Lorde of Cauny ended their liues. The next of kynne [The boy's
to the lord of Cauny chalenged the enheritaunse, whiche legitimacy
was worth foure thousande crounes a yere, alledgyng that tiond ;
the boye was a bastard : and the kynred of the mothers
side, for to saue her honesty, it plainly denied. In conclusion, this matter was in contencion before the Presi- [and at the
dentes of the parliament of Paris, and there hang in he was 8,
controuersie till the child came to the age of eight yeres
old. At which tyme it was demaunded of hym openly
[*p.* 145] whose sonne he was : his frendes of his mothers
side aduertised him to require a day, to be aduised of so

---

[1] It was at this siege that Lord Salisbury and Sir Thos. Gargrave
were kild by the son of the French Master Gunner, as told by Hall,
p. 145, and in 1 *Henry VI*, Act I, sc. iv, l. 69, 71.

great an answer; whiche he asked, & to hym it was grau*n*ted. In y*e* meane season, his said frendes persuaded him to claime his inheritaunce, as sonne to the Lorde of Cawny, which was an honorable liuyng, and an auncie*n*t patrimony; affirming, that if he said contrary, he not only slau*n*dered his mother, shamed himself, & stained his bloud, but also should haue no liuyng, nor any thing to take to. The scholemaster, thinkyng *tha*t his disciple had well learned his lesson, and would reherse it accord- [the boy told the Judges] yng to his instruccio*n*, brought hym before the Iudges at the daie assigned; and when the question was repeted to hym again, he boldly answered, 'my harte geueth me, & [that he was the Duke's Bastard, and not the coward Lord Cauny's son.] my noble corage telleth me, that I am the sonne of the noble Duke of Orleaunce; more glad to be his Bastarde, with a meane liuyng, then the lawfull sonne of that coward cuckolde Cawny, with his foure thousand crounes' [a year].

"The Iustices muche merueiled at his bolde answere; and his mothers cosyns detested him for shamyng of his mother; and his fathers supposed[1] kinne reioysed in [The Duke of Orleans adopted and endowd the boy:] gainyng the patrimony and possessions. Charles, duke of Orleance, heryng of this iudgem*e*nt, toke hym into his family, & gaue him great offices & fees, which he well deserued, for (duryng his [the Duke's] captiuitie) he [the [and he drove out the Eng- lish.] Bastard] defe*n*ded his [the Duke's] la*n*des, expulsed thenglishmen, & in conclusion procured his deliueraunce."

For his first Scene then, the old Playwright borrowd only the death of Richard I, the succession of John, supported by his Mother, the opposition of Arthur backt by Philip II, with demands for cession of territory by John to both Philip and Arthur; and for the Falconbridge part, the possible hint of the Orleans narrative in Hall.

For Scenes ii and iv of Pt. I, the Playwright had only the follow- ing accounts of the Siege of Angiers in 1199 and 1206, and the negotiations for the marriage of Lewes and Blanche in 1200:—

A.D. 1199. (*Hol.* iii. 158/2.) 'In the meane time his mother queene Elianor, togither with capteine Marchades, entred into Aniou, and wasted the same, bicause they of that countrie The city of Angiers taken. had receiued Arthur for their soueraigne lord and gouer- nour.[2] And amongst other townes and fortresses, they tooke 1206 the citie of Angiers, slue manie of the citizens, and com- *Anno Reg.* 8. *Les annales de France.* *Polydor.* mited the rest to prison.' (170/1, 27) 'Finallie he [K. John] entred into Aniou, and comming to the citie of Angiers, appointed certeine bands of his footmen, & all his light horssem*e*n to compasse the towne about, whilest he, with the residue of the footmen, & all the men of armes, did go

[1] ? supposed father's. (On Falconbridge, see p. xxxix, below.)
[2] See p. iv above; and John's capture of the town, mentiond on p. vi.

to assault the gates. Which enterprise with fire and sword
he so manfullie executed, that the gates being in a moment
broken open, the citie was entered and deliuered to the
souldiers for a preie. So that of the citizens some were
taken, some killed, and the wals of the citie beaten flat to
the ground. This doone, he went abroad into the countrie,
and put all things that were in his way to the like destruction. Then came the people of the countries next adioin-
ing, of their owne accord to submit themselues vnto him,
promising to aid him with men and vittals most plentifullie.'

(161/1, 53) 'Finallie vpon the Ascension day in this
second yeare of his [John's] reigne, they came eftsoones to
a communication betwixt the townes of Vernon and Lisle
Dandelie, where finallie they concluded an agreement, with
a marriage to be had betwixt Lewes the sonne of king Philip,
and the ladie Blanch, daughter to Alfonso king of Castile
the 8 of that name, & neece to K. Iohn by his sister El'anor.

'In consideration whereof, king John, besides the
summe of thirtie thousand markes in siluer, as in respect
of dowrie assigned to his said neece, resigned his title to
the citie of Eureux, and also vnto all those townes which
the French king had by warre taken from him, the citie
of Angiers onelie excepted, which citie he receiued againe
by couenants of the same agreement. The French king
restored also to king Iohn (as *Rafe Niger* writeth) the
citie of Tours, and all the castels and fortresses which he
had taken within Touraine : and moreouer, receiued of
king Iohn his homage for all the lands, sees and tene-
ments which at anie time his brother king Richard, or
his father king Henrie had holden of him, the said king
Lewes[1] or any his predecessors, the quit claims and
marriages alwaies excepted. The king of England likewise did homage vnto the French king for Britaine, and
againe (as after you shall heare) receiued homage for the
same countrie, and for the countie of Richmont of his
nephue Arthur. He also gaue the earledome of Glocester
vnto the earle of Eureux, as it were by way of exchange,
for that he resigned to the French king all right, title &
claime that might be pretended to the countie of Eureux.

'By this conclusion of marriage betwixt the said Lewes
and Blanch, the right of king Iohn went awaie, which he
lawfullie before pretended vnto the citie of Eureux, and
vnto those townes in the confines of Berrie, Chateau
Roux or Raoul, Cressie and Isoldune, and likewise vnto
the countrie of Veuxin or Veulquessine, which is a part
of the territorie of Gisors : the right of all which lands,

Marginal notes:

King Iohn won the citie of Angiers by assault [in 1200].

A. D. 1200. *Anno. Reg.* 2. [May 18]

A peace concluded with a marriage.

Matth. Paris. [Blanche's dowry.]

[Angiers is restored to John.]

Ra. Niger.

[I. that is, Philip II.]

[John gives up Evreux, and many other towns.]

Polydor.

townes and countries was released to the king of France by K. John, who supposed that by his affinitie, and resignation of his right to those places, the peace now made would haue continued for euer. And in consideration

The king cometh back again into England.

thereof, he procured furthermore, that the foresaid Blanch should be conueied into France to hir husband with all speed. That doone, he returned into England.'

The 'will', which Eleanor 'can inferre' against Arthur's claim, Part I, sc. ii, l. 98, was made by Richard I., who, in April, 1199 (*Hol.* iii. 155/2, l. 68),

He ordeineth his testament.

'seeing himselfe to wax weaker and weaker, preparing his mind to death, which he perceiued now to be at hand, he ordeined his testament, or rather reformed and added sundrie things vnto the same which he before had made, at the time of his going forth towards the holie land.

[' fealtie]

'Vnto his brother Iohn he assigned the crowne of England, and all other his lands and dominions, causing the Nobles there present to sweare fealtie [1] vnto him ' . . .

For Scenes iii and vi of Part I, the old Playwright had only this bit in *Holinshed*, iii. 160/2, l. 70 :—

Philip king Richards bastard son kills the vicount of Limoges.

'The same yere Philip, bastard sonne to king Richard, to whome his father had giuen the castell and honor of Coinacke, killed the vicount of Limoges,[1] in reuenge of his fathers death, who was slaine (as yee haue heard) in besieging the castell of Chalus Cheuerell.'

For Scene v—the Pandulph part—the old Playwright went to the years 1207-8 and 1211-12 in Holinshed, *Chron.* iii. 171/21, l. 15, and 175/1, l. 7. See below, p. xi—xiii.

The controversy between John and Innocent III., concerning the Pope's appointment of Stephen Langton to the see of Canterbury, began in 1207, when Innocent wrote to John, urging Langton's personal claim to preferment (*Hol.* iii. 171/2, l. 15) :—

A.D. 1207. An. Reg. 8.

[John oppresses all Stephen Langton's supporters.]

'Manie other reasons the pope alledged in his letters to king Iohn, to haue persuaded him to the allowing of the election of Stephan Langton. But king Iohn was so far from giuing care to the popes admonitions, that he with more crueltie handled all such, not onelie of the spiritualtie, but also of the temporaltie, which by any manner means had aided the forenamed Stephan. The pope being hereof aduertised, thought good not to suffer such contempt of his authoritie, as he interpreted it ; namelie, in a matter that touched the iniurious handling

---

[1] He is confused with the Austrich Duke, in the play, and is kild in Part I, Sc. vi, p. 35.

of men within orders of the church. Which example
might procure hinderance, not to one priuat person alone,
but to the whole estate of the spiritualtie, which he would
not suffer in any wise to be suppressed. Wherefore he
decreed with speed to deuise remedie against that large
increasing mischeefe. And though there was no speedier
waie to redresse the same, but by excommunication, yet
he would not vse it at the first towards so mightie a
prince, but gaue him libertie and time to consider his
offense and trespasse so committed.'

[The Pope resolves to check K. John]

As John continued obstinate, he and his realm were interdicted
by the Bishops of London, Ely, and Worcester, acting under
Innocent's order (March 23, 1208), *Hol.* iii. 172/1, l. 25 :—

'Herevpon the said bishops departed, and according
to the popes commission to them sent, vpon the euen of
the Annuntiation of our Ladie, denounced both the king
and the realme of England accursed, and furthermore
caused the doores of churches to be closed vp, and all
other places where diuine seruice was accustomed to
be vsed, first at London, and after in all other places
where they came. Then perceiuing that the K. ment
not to stoope for all this which they had doone, but
rather sought to be reuenged vpon them, they fled the
realme, and got them ouer vnto Stephan the archbishop
of Canturburie, to wit, William bishop of London, Eustace
bishop of Elie, Malger bishop of Worcester, Ioceline bishop
of Bath, and Giles bishop of Hereford.

A.D. 1208.
The mondaie in the passion weeke saith Matth. West.
The king and realm put vnder the popes curse.

'The king taking this matter in verie great displeasure,
seized vpon all their temporalities, and conuerted the
same to his vse, and persecuted such other of the prelacie
as he knew to fauour their dooings, banishing them the
realme, and seizing their goods also into his hands.
Howbeit the most part of the prelats wiselie prouoided
for themselues in this point, so that they would not
depart out of their houses, except they were compelled
by force, which when the kings officers perceiued, they
suffered them to remaine still in their abbies, and other
habitations, bicause they had no commission to vse any
violence in expelling them. But their goods they did
confiscat to the kings vse, allowing them onelie meat and
drinke, and that verie barelie in respect of their former
allowance.

Anno. Reg.
10 1209-10'.
The dealing of the king after the interdiction was pronounced.

'¶ It was a miserable time now for preestes and
churchmen, which were spoiled on euerie hand, without
finding remedie against those that offered them wrong.'

An heauie time for churchmen.

[A.D. 1211.
Hol. iii.
175/1, 7.]
Anno Reg.
13.
Pandulph
and Durant
the Popes
legats.
Polydor.

'In the same yeare also [1211], the pope sent two legats into England, the one named Pandulph a lawier, and the other Durant a templer, who comming vnto king Iohn, exhorted him with manie terrible words to leaue his stubborne disobedience to the church, and to reforme his misdooings. The king for his part quietlie heard them, and bringing them to Northampton, being not farre distant from the place where he met them vpon his returne foorth of Wales had much conference with them; but at length, when they perceiued that they could not haue their purpose, neither for restitution of the goods belonging to preests which he had seized vpon, neither of those that apperteined to certeine other persons, which the king had gotten also into his hands, by meanes of the controuersie betwixt him and the pope, the legats departed, leauing him accursed, and the land interdicted, as they found it at their comming.

[The Legates quit England, leaving John curst and the land interdicted.]
Fabian.
[The Pope's Interdict.]

'¶ Touching the maner of this interdiction there haue beene diuerse opinions, some haue said, that the land was interdicted throughlie, and the churches and houses of religion closed vp, that no where was anie diuine seruice vsed; but it was not so strcit, for there were diuerse places occupied with diuine seruice all that time, by certeine priuiledges purchased either then or before. Children were also christened, and men houseled and annoiled through all the land, except such as were in the bill of excommunication by name expressed.' . . . .

Matth.
Paris.

(Hol. iii. 175/2, l. 17.) 'In the meane time pope Innocent, after the returne of his legats[1] out of England, perceiuing that king Iohn would not be ordered by him, determined with the consent of his cardinals and other councellours, and also at the instant suit of the English bishops and other prelats being there with him, to depriue king Iohn of his kinglie state, and so first absolued all his subiects and vassals of their oths of allegiance made vnto the same king, and after depriued him by solemne protestation of his kinglie administration and dignitie, and lastlie signified that his depriuation vnto the French king and other christian princes, admonishing them to pursue king Iohn, being thus depriued, forsaken, and condemned as a common enimie to God and his church. He ordeined furthermore, that whosoeuer imploied goods or other aid to vanquish and ouercome that disobedient prince, should remaine in assured peace of the church, as well as those which went to visit the sepulchre of our Lord, not onlie in

Polydor.
[The Pope, in 1212,

[deposes John, absolves his subjects from their allegiance,

[and urges K. Philip II. &c. to make war on John.]

[1] Pandulph and Durant.

their goods and persons, but also in suffrages for sauing of
their soules.

'But yet that it might appeare to all men, that nothing
could be more ioifull vnto his holinesse, than to haue
king Iohn to repent his trespasses committed, and to
aske forgiuenesse for the same, he appointed Pandulph, Pandulph
which latelie before was returned to Rome, with a great sent into
France to
number of English exiles, to go into France, togither with practice
Stephan the archbishop of Canturburie, and the other with the
french king,
English bishops, giuing him in commandement, that re- for king Iohn
his destruc-
pairing vnto the French king, he should communicate tion.
with him all that which he had appointed to be doone
against king Iohn, and to exhort the French king to make
warre vpon him, as a person for his wickednesse excommunicated. Moreouer this Pandulph was commanded
by the pope, if he saw cause, to go ouer into England,
and to deliuer vnto king Iohn such letters as the pope
had written for his better instruction, and to seeke by all
means possible to draw him from his naughtie opinion.

(*Hol.* iii. 175/2, l. 57.) 'In the meane time, when it was
bruted through the realme of England, that the pope had
released the people & absolued them of their oth of fidelitie [After the
Pope's Into the king, and that he was depriued of his gouernement by terdict, many
the popes sentence, by little and little a great number both English
migrate to
of souldiers, citizens, burgesses, capteins and conestables France.]
of castels, leauing their charges, & bishops with a great
multitude of preests reuolting from him, and auoiding his
companie and presence, secretlie stale awaie, and got ouer
into France.' . . .

In Sc. v, line 79 (2)—perhaps John's declaration that he will be
supreme head over temporal as well as spiritual, was suggested by
the 2nd paragraph of the following extract (*Hol.* iii. 173/2, l. 58) :—

'¶ There liued in those daies a diuine named Alexander *Anno Reg.*
II (A.D.
Cementarius, surnamed Theologus, who by his preaching 1210-11).
incensed the king greatlie vnto all crueltie (as the monks Cementarius
and friers saie) against his subiects, affirming that the
generall scourge wherewith the people were afflicted,
chanced not through the princes fault, but for the [Justifies
John's
wickednesse of his people, for the king was but the rod cruelty to
of the Lords wrath, and to this end a prince was ordeined, his subjects.]
that he might rule the people with a rod of iron, and
breake them as an earthen vessell, to chaine the mighty
in fetters, & the noble men in iron manacles. . .

'He went about also to prooue with likelie arguments,
that it apperteined not to the pope, to haue to doo con-

[Cementarius
argues
against the
Pope's right
to interfere
in temporal
matters.]

cerning the temporall possessions of any kings or other potentates touching the rule and gouernment of their subiects, sith no power was granted to Peter (the speciall and cheefe of the apostles of the Lord) but onlie touching the church, and matters apperteining therevnto. By such doctrine of him set foorth, he wan in such wise the kings fauour, that he obteined manie great preferments at the kings hands, and was abbat of saint Austines in Canturburie.' . . .

In Scenes vii, viii, ix, allowing for anachronism, the writer of the old play had authority for the capture of Queen Eleanor by Arthur, and her subsequent release by John. *Hol. Chron.* iii. 164/2, l. 13:—

An. Dom.
1202.
Queene
Elianor.

'Queene Elianor that was regent in those parties being put in great feare with the newes of this sudden sturre, got hir into Mirabeau a strong towne, situat in the countrie of Aniou, and forthwith dispatched a messenger with letters vnto king Iohn, requiring him of speedie succour in this

[Arthur
captures Q.
Eleanor.]

hir present danger. In the meane time, Arthur following the victorie, shortlie after followed hir, and woone Mirabeau, where he tooke his grandmother within the same,

Matth.
Paris.
Matth.
West.

whom he yet intreated verie honorablie, and with great reuerence (as some haue reported.) ¶ But other write far more trulie, that she was not taken, but escaped into a tower, within the which she was straitlie besieged. Thither came also to aid Arthur all the Nobles and men of armes in Poictou, and namelie the foresaid carle of March according to appointment betwixt them: so that

[Arthur's
great Army.]

by this meanes Arthur had a great armie togither in the field.

[John de-
nounces K.
Philip II. for
bad faith.]

'King Iohn in the meane time, hauing receiued his mothers letters, and vnderstanding thereby in what danger she stood, was maruellouslie troubled with the strangenesse of the newes, and with manie bitter words accused

Polydor.

the French king as an vntrue prince, and a fraudulent league-breaker: and in all possible hast speedeth him foorth, continuing his iournie for the most part both day

K. Iohn
commeth
vpon his
enimies not
looked for.

and night to come to the succour of his people. To be briefe, he vsed such diligence, that he was vpon his enimies necks yer they could vnderstand any thing of his comming, or gesse what the matter meant, when they saw such a companie of souldiers as he brought with him to approch so neere the citie. For so negligent were they, that hauing once woone the towne, they ranged abroad ouer the countrie hither and thither at their libertie without any care. So that now being put in a sudden feare, as preuented by the hastie comming of the enimies vpon them, and wanting leisure to take aduice what was best to be doone, and hauing not time in manner to get any armour on their backs, they were in a maruellous trouble, not knowing whether it were best for them to fight or to flee, to yeeld or to resist. [Indecision of the French.]

'This their feare being apparent to the Englishmen (by their disorder shewed in running vp and downe from place to place with great noise and turmoile) they set vpon them with great violence, and compassing them round about, they either tooke or slue them in a manner at their pleasure. And hauing thus put them all to flight, they pursued the chase towardes the towne of Mirabeau, into which the enimies made verie great hast to enter: but such speed was vsed by the English souldiers at that present, that they entred and wan the said towne before their enimies could come neere to get into it. Great slaughter was made within Mirabeau it selfe, and Arthur with the residue of the armie that escaped with life from the first bickering was taken, who being herevpon committed to prison, first at Falais, and after within the citie of Rouen, liued not long after as you shall heare. The other of the prisoners were also committed vnto safe keeping, some into castels within Normandie, and some were sent into England.' . . . [The English capture and slay the French, [and take Mirabeau.] Arthur duke of Britaine taken prisoner. Matth. Paris.

Of Scene x of the Play, the joke of the Friars and Nuns is the Playwright's own, from wide popular experience. For the Prophet of Scene x, see p. xviii, below. For Arthur and Hubert in Scene xi, Part I, John's recrowning, the Bastard's 5 Moons, and Arthur's death in Part II, sc. i, and for the wind-up of Part I, Holinshed gave the following material :—

(*Hol.* iii. p. 165, l. 31.) 'The French king at the same time lieng in siege before Arques, immediatly vpon the newes of this ouerthrow, raised from thence, and returned home-wards, destroieng all that came in his waie, till he was entred into his owne countrie. It is said that king Iohn caused his nephue Arthur to be brought before him at Falais, and there went about to persuade him all that he could to for-sake his freendship and aliance with the French king, and to leane and sticke to him being his naturall vncle. But Arthur, like one that wanted good counsell, and abound-ing too much in his owne wilfull opinion, made a pre-sumptuous answer,[1] not onelie denieng so to doo, but also A.D. 1202. Anno Reg. 4. [Arthur before John at Falaise.]

[1] The old playwright has skilfully alterd Arthur's character.

commanding king Iohn to restore vnto him the realme of
England, with all those other lands and possessions which
king Richard had in his hand at the houre of his death.
For sith the same apperteined to him by right of inherit-
ance, he assured him, except restitution were made the
sooner, he should not long continue quiet. King Iohn
being sore mooued with such words thus vttered by his
nephue, appointed (as before is said) that he should be
straitlie kept in prison, as first in Falais, and after at
Roan within the new castell there. Thus by means of
this good successe, the countries of Poictou, Touraine,
and Aniou were recouered.

[John impris ns Arthur at Falaise, and then Rouen.]

'Shortlie after, king Iohn comming ouer into England,
caused himselfe to be crowned againe at Canturburie by
the hands of Hubert the archbishop there, on the four-
teenth day of Aprill, and then went backe againe into
Normandie, where immediatlie vpon his arriuall, a rumour
was spred through all France, of the death of his nephue
Arthur. True it is that great suit was made to haue
Arthur set at libertie, as well by the French king, as by
William de Riches a valiant baron of Poictou, and diuerse
other Noble men of the Britains, who when they could
not preuaile in their suit, they banded themselues togither,
and ioining in confederacie with Robert earle of Alanson,
the vicount Beaumont, William de Fulgiers, and other,
they began to leuie sharpe wars against king Iohn in
diuerse places, insomuch (as it was thought) that so long
as Arthur liued, there would be no quiet in those parts:
where[1]upon it was reported, that king Iohn, through per-
suasion of his councellors, appointed certeine persons to
go vnto Falais, where Arthur was kept in prison, vnder
the charge of Hubert de Burgh, and there to put out the
yoong gentlemans eies. [Part I, sc. xi. of the Play.]

Matth. Paris. King John eftsoones crowned. A.D. 1203.

Rafe Cog.

[John orders Arthur's eyes to be put out.]

'But through such resistance as he made against one
of the tormentors that came to execute the kings commandement (for the other rather forsooke their prince
and countrie, than they would consent to obeie the kings
authoritie heerein) and such lamentable words as he
vttered, Hubert de Burgh did preserue him from that
iniurie, not doubting but rather to haue thanks than displeasure at the kings hands, for deliuering him of such
infamie as would haue redounded vnto his highnesse, if
the yoong gentleman had beene so cruellie dealt withall.
For he considered, that king Iohn had resolued vpon this
point onelie in his heat and furie (which moueth men to

[Arthur pleads for his sight. Hubert de Burgh saves it.]

[1] *Hol.* iii. p. 165, col. 2.

vndertake manie an inconuenient enterprise, vnbesceem- [Hubert's motives in sparing Arthur.]
ing the person of a common man, much more reproch-
full to a prince, all men in that mood being meere foolish
and furious, and prone to accomplish the puruerse conceits
of their ill possessed heart ; as one saith right well,

——————*pronus in iram*
Stultorum est animus, facilè excandescit, & audet
Omne scelus, quoties concepta bile tumescit)

and that afterwards, vpon better aduisement, he would
both repent himselfe so to haue commanded, and giue
them small thanke that should see it put in execution.
Howbeit to satisfie his mind for the time, and to staie [Hubert spreads a report of Arthur's death.]
the rage of the Britains, he caused it to be bruted abroad
through the countrie, that the kings commandement was
fulfilled, and that Arthur also through sorrow and greefe
was departed out of this life. For the space of fifteene
daies this rumour incessantlie ran through both the realmes
of England and France, and there was ringing for him
through townes and villages, as it had beene for his funerals.
It was also bruted, that his bodie was buried in the mon-
asterie of saint Andrewes of the Cisteaux order.

'But when the Britains were nothing pacified, but [Anger of the Bretons at it.]
rather kindled more vehementlie to worke all the mis-
cheefe they could deuise, in reuenge of their souereignes
death, there was no remedie but to signifie abroad againe,
that Arthur was yet liuing and in health.   Now when the [Arthur reported to be alive and well.]
king heard the truth of all this matter, he was nothing dis-
pleased for that his commandement was not executed,
sith there were diuerse of his capteins which vttered in
plaine words, that he should not find knights to keepe his
castels, if he dealt so cruellie with his nephue.   For if it
chanced any of them to be taken by the king of France
or other their aduersaries, they should be sure to tast of
the like cup.   ¶ But now touching the maner in verie
deed of the end of this Arthur[1], writers make sundrie
reports. Neuerthelesse certeine it is, that in the yeare
next insuing, he was remooued from Falais vnto the [Arthur, in prison at Rouen, is said
castell or tower of Rouen, out of the which there was not
any that would confesse that euer he saw him go aliue.
Some haue written, that as he assaied to haue escaped out
of prison, and proouing to clime ouer the wals of the [to have climbd the walls, and been drownd,
castell, he fell into the riuer of Saine, and so was drowned.
Other write, that through verie greefe and languor he
pined awaie, and died of naturall sicknesse. But some
affirme, that king Iohn secretlie caused him to be mur-

[1] This takes us to Part II, sc. i, of the old Play.

[or murderd by John's order.] thered and made awaie, so as it is not throughlie agreed vpon, in what sort he finished his daies: but verelie king Iohn was had in great suspicion, whether worthilie or not, the lord knoweth.' . . . .

(The old Playwright wisely didn't notice Constance's re-marriage and her accusation of K. John (*Hol.* iii. 166/1) :—

Guie son to the vicount of Touars. [Marries Constance.] 'The Lord Guie, sonne to the vicount of Touars, who had taken Arthurs mother Constance to wife, after the diuorse made betwixt hir and the earle of Chester, in right of hir obteined the dukedome of Britaine. But king Philip after he was aduertised of Arthurs death, tooke the matter verie greeuouslie, and vpon occasion therof, cited king Iohn to appeare before him at a certeine day, to answer such obiections as Constance the duches of Britaine mother to the said Arthur should lay to his charge, touching the murther of hir sonne. And bicause king Iohn appeared not, he was therefore condemned in the action, and adiudged to forfeit all that he held within the precinct of France, aswell Normandie as all his other lands and dominions.')

Constance, the mother of duke Arthur, accuseth king Iohn.

For the 5 Moons in Sc. xii of the Play, Part I (A.D. 1202), Holinshed gives the following, under 1200 (*Hol.* iii. 163/1, l. 45) :—

Fiue moones.   A.D. 1200. 'About the moneth of December, there were scene in the prouince of Yorke fiue moones, one in the east, the second in the west, the third in the north, the fourth in the south, and the fift as it were set in the middest of the other, hauing manie stars about it, and went fiue or six times incompassing the other, as it were the space of one houre, and shortlie after vanished awaie.'

We now come to Scene ii of Part II, p. 8, John and the Prophet.

For 'Peter, a Prophet, with people' in Part I, Scene xi, p. 43-4, and his talk with K. John in Sc. xiii, p. 52-4 (A.D. 1202), in which he prophesies John's loss of his Crown before Ascension-day, and also for Peter's appearance in Part II, Sc. ii, p. 9, Holinshed has only the following, under the year 1213-14 (it should be 1212: see Matthew Paris), *Chron.* iii. 180, col. i, line 18.

An hermit named Peter of Pontfret, or Wakefield as some writers haue. See M. *Fea*, [some first, *pag.* 331.] 'There was in this season an heremit, whose name was Peter, dwelling about Yorke, a man in great reputation with the common people, bicause that either inspired with some spirit of prophesie as the people beleeued, or else hauing some notable skill in art magike, he was accustomed to tell what should follow after. And for

so much as oftentimes his saiengs prooued true, great
credit was giuen to him as to a verie prophet . . . .
. . . 'This Peter, about the first of Ianuarie last past, had [Peter pro-phesied that John would be cast out of England before Ascension Day.]
told the king, that at the feast of the Ascension it should
come to passe, that he should be cast out of his kingdome.
And (whether, to the intent that his words should be the
better beleeued, or whether vpon too much trust of his
owne cunning) he offered himselfe to suffer death for it, if
his prophesie prooued not true. Herevpon being committed to prison within the castell of Corfe, when the day [Hol. Torf]
by him prefixed came, without any other notable damage
vnto king Iohn, he was by the kings commandement The heremit and his sonne hanged.
drawne from the said castell, vnto the towne of Warham,
& there hanged, togither with his sonne.
    'The people much blamed king Iohn, for this extreame [The people blame John,
dealing, bicause that the heremit was supposed to be a
man of great vertue, and his sonne nothing guiltie of the
offense committed by his father (if any were) against the
king. Moreouer, some thought, that he had much wrong
to die, bicause the matter fell out euen as he had pro-
phesied : for the day before the Ascension day, king Iohn [as he did resign his kingdom to the Pope before Ascension Day.]
had resigned the superioritie of his kingdome (as they
tooke the matter) vnto the pope, and had doone to him
homage, so that he was no absolute king indeed, as
authors affirme. One cause, and that not the least which
mooued king Iohn the sooner to agree with the pope,
rose through the words of the said heremit, that did put
such a feare of some great mishap in his hart, which
should grow through the disloialtie of his people, that it
made him yeeld the sooner.'

    The death of Q. Eleanor in 1204 is not noted by the Playwright
till Part II, sc. ii, l. 118-120, p. 12, in 1214, as if it had then just
happened :—

    (*Hol.* iii. 167/2, l. 73.) 'About this time [1204] queene A.D. 1204.
Elianor the mother of king Iohn departed this life, con-
sumed rather through sorow and anguish of mind, than of
any other naturall infirmitie.'

    In 1214 John, then in France, inuaded Britany, but fearing
Lewes's army, retreated to Angiers, and remained there while Lewes
subdued the Poitevins, and his father, K. Philip II., beat the united
Flemish, German, and English forces, under the Emperor Otho, at
the bridge of Bouvines, on July 26 (27, Mat. Paris), 1214, a defeat
which was disastrous to John (*Hol.* iii. 183, col. 2, l. 4) :—

'Now king Iohn being aduertised of that ouerthrow, was maruellouslie sad and sorrowfull for the chance, in somuch that he would not receiue any meat in a whole daie after the newes thereof was brought vnto him. At length turning his sorrow into rage, he openlie said, that since the time that he made himselfe & his kingdom subiect to the church of Rome, nothing that he did had prospered well with him. Indeed he condescended to an agreement with the pope (as may be thought) more by force than of deuotion, and therefore rather dissembled with the pope (sith he could not otherwise choose) than agreed to the couenants with any hartie affection.

The saieng of king Iohn. [Nothing had prospered with him since he submitted to the Pope.]

'But to the purpose. Perceiuing himselfe now destitute of his best freends, of whom diuerse remained prisoners with the French king (being taken at the battell of Bouins) he thought good to agree with king Philip for this present, by way of taking some truce, which by mediation of ambassadours riding to and fro betwixt them, was at length accorded to endure for fiue yeares, and to begin at Easter, in the yeare of our Lord, 1215. After this, about the 19 daie of October he returned into England, to appease certeine tumults which began alreadie to shoot out buds of some new ciuill dissention. And suerlie the same spred abroad their blossoms so freshlie, that the fruit was knit before the growth by anie timelie prouision could be hindered. For the people being set on by diuerse of the superiours of both sorts, finding themselues greeued that the king kept not promise in restoring the ancient lawes of S. Edward, determined from thenceefoorth to vse force, since by request he might not preuaile.'. .

A truce taken betwixt the two kings of England & France.

[The English people determine to vse force against John.]

We must now hark back to the end of Scene i, Part II, the resolve of the rebel English Nobles, after Arthur's death, to ask the Dolphin of France to enter England and claim the throne, and to meet at Bury St. Edmunds, on April 10, to confer, and to aid Lewes in his enterprise, l. 81-108, p. 7-8, below. With this, we will take the Bastard's speech, l. 73-87 of Sc. ii, Pt. II, p. 10-11 below, and Part II, Scene iii, p. 15 below, the meeting of these Nobles at Bury; and we may fairly conclude that Essex's first line in the Play, ' Under the cloke of holie Pilgrimage,' came from the Holinshed side-note, ' A cloked pilgrimage.' But the old Playwright has reverst Holinshed's order of events, and has made the sending for the Dolphin come before, instead of after, the meeting at Bury. The old Playwright has also alterd the motive of the Nobles' pilgrimage. Holinshed says, iii. 183, col. 2, l. 45 :—

'The Nobles, supposing that longer delaie therein was
not to be suffered, assembled themselues togither at the
abbeie of Burie (vnder colour of going thither to doe
their deuotions to the bodie of S. Edmund which laie
there inshrined) where they vttered their complaint of
the kings tyrannicall maners.' . . . . . [and where was read
to them a charter of Henry I, confirming Edward the
Confessor's grant of certain liberties].

(l. 74) 'And therefore being thus assembled in the queere
of the church of S. Edmund, they receiued a solemne oth
vpon the altar there, that if the king would not grant to
the same liberties, with others which he of his owne
accord had promised to confirme to them, they would
from thencefoorth make warre vpon him, till they had
obteined their purpose, and inforced him to grant, not
onelie to all these their petitions, but also yeeld to the
confirmation of them vnder his seale, for euer to remaine
most stedfast and inuiolable.'

In 1215 the Barons wrest Magna Charta—an incident which
no dramatist would dare put on the stage in Elizabeth's time—from
John, but the Pope takes his side, annuls the Charter, and excom-
municates the Barons, who resolue to settle their quarrel by the
sword. John, however, prevails against them, and then, says Holinshed, iii. 190, col. 1, l. 43, A.D. 1216 :—

'The barons of the realme being thus afflicted with
so manie mischeefes all at one time, as both by the
sharpe and cruell warres which the king made against
them on the one side, and by the enmitie of the pope on
the other side, they knew not which way to turne them,
nor how to seeke for releefe. For by the losse of their
complices taken in the castell of Rochester, they saw not
how it should any thing auaile them to ioine in battell
with the king. Therefore considering that they were in
such extremitie of despaire, they resolued with themselues
to seeke for aid at the enimies hands, and there vpon
Saer earle of Winchester, and Robert Fitz Walter, with
letters vnder their seales, were sent vnto Lewes, the sonne
of Philip the French king, offering him the crowne of
England, and sufficient pledges for performance of the
same, and other couenants to be agreed betwixt them,
requiring him with all speed to come vnto their succour.
This Lewes had married (as before is said) Blanch,
daughter to Alfonse king of Castile, neece to king Iohn
by his sister Elianor.

A cloked
pilgrimage.

[The English
nobles meet
at Bury St.
Edmund's,

[and swear
to make war
on John if
he'll not
grant their
liberties.]

[The English
nobles are
afflicted by
John's vic-
tories over
them, and by
the Pope's
enmity.]

The lords
send to the
French kings
sonne, offer-
ing to him
the crowne.

[Philip II. promises to invade England.] 'Now king Philip the father of this Lewes, being glad to haue such an occasion to inuade the relme of England, which he neuer looued, promised willinglie that his sonne should come vnto the aid of the said barons with all con-uenient speed (but first he receiued foure and twentie hostages, which he placed at Campaine for further assur-ance of the couenants accorded) and herewith he pre-pared an armie, and diuerse ships to transport his sonne and his armie ouer into England. In the meane time, and to put the barons in comfort, he sent ouer a certeine [p. 190, col. 2] number of armed men, vnder the leading of the chate-French men sent ouer to the aid of the barons. laine of saint Omers and the chatelaine of Arras, Hugh Thacon, Eustace de Neuille, Baldwin Brecell, William de Winnes, Giles de Melun[1], W. de Beamont, Giles de Hersie, Biset de Fersie, and others, the which taking the sea, arriued with one and fortie ships in the Thames, and so The satur-day after the Epiphanie, saith R'afe C'eg. came to London the seauen and twentith of Februarie, where they were receiued of the barons with great ioy and gladnesse. Moreouer the said Lewes wrote to the barons, that he purposed by Gods assistance to be at Calice by a day appointed, with an armie redie to passe ouer with all speed vnto their succours.' [p. 190, l. 13 : for l. 69 &c. see p. xxiv, at foot.]

We go back now to the entrance of Pandulph in Part II, Scene ii, of the Play, p. 13, and to the year 1213, and Holinshed's *Chronicle*, iii. 176/2, l. 18.

1213.
The French king pre-pared to inuade England. 'Ye shall vnderstand, the French king being requested by Pandulph the popes legat, to take the warre in hand against king Iohn, was easilie persuaded thereto of an inward hatred that he bare vnto our king, and therevpon with all diligence made his prouision of men, ships, munition and vittell, in purpose to passe ouer into Eng-land : and now was his nauie readie rigged at the mouth of Saine, and he in greatest forwardnesse, to take his iournie. When Pandulph vpon good considerations thought first to go eftsoones, or at the least wise to send into England, before the French armie should land there, and to assaie once againe, if he might induce the king to [John pre-pared to resist him.] shew himselfe reformable vnto the popes pleasure : king Iohn, hauing knowledge of the French kings purpose and ordinance, assembled his people, and lodged with them alongst by the coast towards France, that he might resist his enimies, and keepe them off from landing.' . . . .

---

[1] The 'Vicount Meloun' of Part II, Sc. iii, and Sc. v. of the Play, p. 22, 26.

Then follows the material for Scene iv of Pt. II, p. 24, John's surrender of his Crown to the Pope's legate, and his agreement to hold his kingdom thenceforth of the Pope. (The extracts for Sc. iii, the oath on the Altar, p. 19, and Lewes's coming, p. 20, are on p. xxi above and p. xxvii below.)

(*Hol.* iii. 176/2, l. 65.) ' But as he lay thus readie, neere to the coast, to withstand and beat backe his enimies, there arriued at Douer two Templers, who comming before the king, declared vnto him that they were sent from Pandulph the popes legat, who for his profit coueted to talke with him: for he had (as they affirmed) meanes to propone, whereby he might be reconciled, both to God and his church, although he were adiudged in the court of Rome, to haue forfeited all the right which he had to his kingdome. [Pandulph's proposal to reconcile John with the Pope.]

'The king vnderstanding the meaning of the messengers, sent them backe againe to bring ouer the legat, who incontinentlie came ouer to Douer, of whose arriuall when the king was aduertised, he went thither, and receiued him with all due honour and reuerence.' [The legat Pandulph cometh ouer.]

Here follows a 'sawcie speech of proud Pandulph the popes lewd legat, to king Iohn, in the presumptuous popes behalfe;' which the dramatist has not used.

(*Hol.* iii. 177/1, l. 60.) ' These words being thus spoken by the legat, king Iohn as then vtterlie despairing in his matters, when he saw himselfe constreined to obeie, was in a great perplexitie of mind, and as one full of thought, looked about him with a frowning countenance, waieng with himselfe what counsell were best for him to follow. At length, oppressed with the burthen of the imminent danger and ruine, against his will, and verie loth so to haue doone, he promised vpon his oth to stand to the popes order and decree. Wherefore shortlie after (in like manner as pope Innocent had commanded) he tooke the crowne from his owne head, and deliuered the same to Pandulph the legat, neither he, nor his heires at anie time thereafter to receiue the same, but at the popes hands. Upon this, he promised to receiue Stephan the archbishop of Canturburie into his fauour, with all other the bishops and banished men, making vnto them sufficient amends for all iniuries to them doone, and so to pardon them, that they should not run into any danger, for that they had rebelled against him. [Despair and hesitation of K. John.] [K. Iohn deliuereth his crowne vnto Pandulph.]

'Then Pandulph keeping the crowne with him for the [Pandulph

restoreth
the crowne
aga.n to the
kinge.

space of fiue daies in token of possession thereof, at length
(as the popes vicar) gaue it him againe. By means of this
act (saith Polydor) the fame went abroad, that king Iohn
willing to continue the memorie hereof, made himselfe
vassall to pope Innocent, with condition, that his succes-

[To hold
England of
the Pope.]

sors should likewise from thenceefoorth acknowledge to
haue their right to the same kingdome from the pope.
But those kings that succeeded king Iohn, haue not

Ran.
Higden.

obserued any such lawes of reconciliation, neither doo
the autentike chronicles of the realme make mention of
any such surrender, so that such articles as were appointed
to king Iohn to obserue, perteined vnto him that had
offended, and not to his successors. Thus saith Polydor'. .

Holinshed gives John's Charter of submission and words of
fealty to the Pope, and adds, iii. 178, col. 2, l. 34 :—

1213.

[Pandulph
gets 8000
marks from
K. John,
and gues to
K. Philip II.]

'Pandulph hauing thus reconciled king Iohn, thought
not good to release the excommunication, till the king
had performed all things which he had promised, and so
with all speed hauing receiued eight thousand markes
sterling in part of restitution to be made to the archbishop, and the other banished men, he sailed backe into
France, & came to Roan, where he declared to king Philip
the effect of his trauell, and what he had doone in England. But king Philip hauing in this meane while con-
sumed a great masse of monie, to the summe of sixtie
thousand pounds, as he himselfe alledged, about the
furniture of his iournie, which he intended to haue made
into England, vpon hope to haue had no small aid within
the realme, by reason of such bishops and other banished

[Philip II.
will not give
up the
invasion of
England.]

men as he had in France with him, was much offended
for the reconciliation of king Iohn, and determined not
so to breake off his enterprise, least it might be imputed
to him for a great reproch to haue beene at such charges
and great expenses in vaine. Therefore calling his councell togither, he declared vnto them what he purposed
to doo.'

We now take up the Chronicle from p. xxii, above, before the
Pandulph incident. In 1215 John returnd from the borders of
Scotland, and threatend to besiege London, but withdrew on finding the Citizens ready to fight. The navy he had prepared to
encounter Lewes, was disperst by tempest, and, says Holinshed, iii.
190, col. 2, l. 69, John :—

King John
once againe

'Somewhat before this time also, when he heard of the
compact made betwixt the barons and his aduersaries the

Frenchmen, he dispatched a messenger in all hast to *sendeth to the pope.* the pope, signifieng to him what was in hand and practised against him, requiring furthermore the said pope by his authoritie to cause Lewes to staie his iournie, and to succour those rebels in England which he had alreadie excommunicated.' . . .

For Scene iv of Part II, lines 19-78 (p. 24-6), Pandulph's attempt (near Bury) to withdraw Lewes and the French from the invasion of England, Holinshed gave the old Playwright an account of a first attempt in France, and a second later one in England, p. xxviii.

'The pope desirous to helpe king Iohn all that he *Anno Reg.* might (bicause he was now his vassall) sent his legat *18.* Gualo into France, to disswade king Philip from taking *[A.D. 1216.]* *Cardinall* anie enterprise in hand against the king of England. *Gualo.* But king Philip, though he was content to heare what the *Matth. Paris.* legat could saie, yet by no meanes would be turned from *The French* the execution of his purpose, alledging that king Iohn *kings allega-* was not the lawfull king of England, hauing first vsurped *tions to the* and taken it awaie from his nephue Arthur the lawfull *popes legat Gualo.* inheritour, and that now sithens as an enimie to his owne roiall dignitie he had giuen the right of his kingdome awaie to the pope (which he could not doo without con- *Matth.* sent of his nobles) and therefore through his owne fault *West.* he was worthilie depriued of all his kinglie honor. For the kingdome of England (saith he) neuer belonged to *Matth.* the patrimonie of S. Peter, nor at anie time shall. For *Paris.* admit that he were rightfull king, yet neither he nor anie other prince may giue awaie his kingdome without the assent of his barons, which are bound to defend the same, and the prerogatiue roiall, to the vttermost of their powers. Furthermore (saith he) if the pope doo meane to main- teine this errour, he shall giue a perilous example to all kingdomes of the world. Herewithall the Nobles of France then present, protested also with one voice, that in defense of this article they would stand to the death, which is, that no king or prince at his will and pleasure might giue awaie his kingdome, or make it tributarie to anie other potentate, whereby the Nobles should become thrall or subiect to a forren gouernour. These things were doone at Lions in the quindene after Easter.

'Lewes on the morrow following, being the 26 of Aprill, *Lewes, the* by his fathers procurement, came into the councell chamber, *French kings* and with frowning looke beheld the legat, where by his pro- *sonne, main-* curator he defended the cause that moued him to take *teineth his* vpon him this iournie into England, disprouing not onelie *pretended title to the crowne of England.*

the right which king Iohn had to the crowne, but also alledging his owne interest, not onelie by his new election of the barons, but also in the title of his wife, whose mother the queene of Castile remained onelie aliue of all the brethren and sisters of Henrie the second late king of England (as before ye haue heard.) The legat made answer herevnto, "that king Iohn had taken vpon him the crosse, as one appointed to go to warre against Gods enimies in the holie land, wherefore he ought by decree of the generall councell to haue peace for foure yeares to come, and to remaine in suertie vnder protection of the apostolike see." But Lewes replied thereto, that king Iohn had by warre first inuaded his castels and lands in Picardie, and wasted the same, as Buncham castell and Liens, with the countie of Guisnes which belonged to the see of the said Lewes.

'But these reasons notwithstanding, the legat warned the French king on paine of cursing, not to suffer his sonne to go into England, and likewise his sonne, that he should not presume to take the iournie in hand. But Lewes hearing this, declared that his [1] father had nothing to do to forbid him to prosecute his right in the realme of England, which was not holden of him, and therefore required his father not to hinder his purpose in such things as belonged nothing to him, but rather to licence him to seeke the recouerie of his wiues right, which he meant to pursue with perill of life, if need should require.

'The legat perceiuing he could not preuaile in his sute made to king Philip, thought that he would not spend time longer in vaine, in further treating with him, but sped him foorth into England, obteining yet a safeconduct of the French king to passe through his realme. Lewes in like maner, purposing by all meanes to preuent [2] the legat, first dispatched foorth ambassadours in all hast vnto the court of Rome to excuse himselfe to the pope, and to render the reasons that most speciallie mooued him to proceed forward in his enterprise against king Iohn, being called by the barons of England to take the crowne thereof vpon him. This doone, with all conuenient speed he came downe to Calice, where he found 680 ships well appointed and trimmed, which Eustace surnamed the monke had gathered and prepared there readie against his comming.

'Lewes therefore foorthwith imbarking himselfe with his people, and all necessarie prouisions for such a iournie,

[1] page 191, col. 2. [2] be before, forestall.

tooke the sea, and arriued at a place called Stanchorre in *He taketh the sea.*
the Ile of Tenet, vpon the 21 day of Maie, and shortlie
after came to Sandwich, & there landed with all his people, *He landeth in Kent.*
where he also incamped vpon the shore by the space of
three daies. In which meane time there came vnto him
a great number of those lords and gentlemen which had *The Lords doo homage vnto him.*
sent for him, and there euerie one apart and by himselfe
sware fealtie and homage vnto him, as if he had beene
their true and naturall prince.

'King John about the same time that Lewes thus
arriued, came to Douer, meaning to fight with his aduersaries by the way as they should come ·forward towards
London. But yet vpon other aduisement taken, he
changed his purpose, bicause he put some doubt in the
Flemings and other strangers, of whome the most part of *Matth. Paris.*
his armie consisted, bicause he knew that they hated the
Frenchmen no more than they did the English. There-
fore furnishing the castell of Douer, with men, munition, *Hubert de Burgh.*
and vittels, he left it in the keeping of Hubert de Burgh,
a man of notable prowesse & valiancie, and returned himselfe vnto Canturburie, and from thence tooke the high
waie towards Winchester. Lewes being aduertised that
king Iohn was retired out of Kent, passed through the
countrie without anie incounter, and wan all the castels
and holds as he went, but Douer he could not win.

'At his comming to Rochester, he laid siege to the *Rochester castell woone.*
castell there, and wan it, causing all the strangers that
were found within it to be hanged. This doone, he came
to London, and there receiued the homage of those lords *Lewes com-meth to London.*
and gentlemen which had not yet doone their homage to
him at Sandwich. On the other part he tooke an oth to
mainteine and performe the old lawes and customes of
the realme, and to restore to euerie man his rightfull
heritage and lands, requiring the barons furthermore to
continue faithfull towards him, assuring them to bring *[He swears to grant the barons their ancient liberties.]*
things so to passe, that the realme of England should
recouer the former dignitie, and they their ancient liberties.
Moreouer he vsed them so courteouslie, gaue them so faire
words, and made such large promises, that they beleeued
him with all their harts. But alas! *Cur vincit opinio*
verum?

'The rumour of this pretended outward courtesie being
once spred through the realme, caused great numbers of *[Many folk flock to Lewes.]*
people to come flocking to him, among [1]whome were
diuerse of those which before had taken part with king

[1] page 192, col. 1.

Iohn, as William earle Warren, William earle of Arundell, William earle of Salisburie, William Marshall the yoonger, and diuerse other, supposing verelie that the French kings sonne should now obteine the kingdome, who in the meane

time ordeined Simon Langton afore mentioned, to be his chancellour, by whose preaching and exhortation, as well the citizens of London as the barons that were excommunicated, caused diuine seruice to be celebrated in their presence, induced thereto, bicause Lewes had alreadie sent his procurators to Rome before his comming into England, there to shew the goodnesse of his cause and quarell.

'But this auailed them not, neither tooke his excuse any such effect as he did hope it should : for those ambassadors that king Iohn had sent thither, replied against their assertions, so that there was hard hold about it in that court, albeit that the pope would decree nothing till he hard further from his legat Gualo, who the same time

(being aduertised of the proceedings of Lewes in his iournie) with all diligence hasted ouer into England, and passing through the middle of his aduersaries, came vnto king Iohn, then soiourning at Glocester, of whome he was most ioifullie receiued, for in him king Iohn reposed

all his hope of victorie. This legat immediatlie after his comming did excommunicate Lewes by name, with all his fautors and complices, but speciallie Simon de Langton, with bell, booke, and candle, as the maner was. Howbeit the same Simon, and one Geruase de Hobrug deane of S. Pauls in London, with other, alledged that for the right and state of the cause of Lewes, they had alreadie appealed to the court of Rome, and therefore the sentence published by Gualo they tooke as void.'

Nearly the whole south of England, with Essex and Suffolk, took Lewes's side ; and, says Holinshed, iii. 192, col. 2, l. 26 :—

'About the feast of saint Margaret, Lewes with the lords came againe to London, at whose comming, the tower of London was yeelded vp to him by appointment, after which the French capteins and gentlemen, thinking themselues assured of the realme, began to shew their inward dispositions and hatred toward the Englishmen,

and forgetting all former promises (such is the nature of strangers, and men of meane estate, that are once become lords of their desires, according to the poets words,

Asperius nihil est humili cùm surgit altum)

they did manie excessiue outrages, in spoiling and rob-

bing the people of the countrie, without pitie or mercie.
Moreouer they did not onelie breake into mens houses, [The French
but also into churches, and tooke out of the same such soldiers
vessels and ornaments of gold and siluer, as they could lish men and
laie hands vpon : for Lewes had not the power now to churches,
rule the greedie souldiers, being wholie giuen to the spoile.

'But most of all their tyrannie did appeare in the east
parts of the realme, when they went through the countries [specially in
of Essex, Suffolke and Northfolke, where they miserablie counties.]
spoiled the townes and villages, reducing those quarters
vnder their subiection, and making them tributaries vnto
Lewes in most seruile and slauish manner.'

For Scene v of Part II (p. 26-8), Meloun's dying disclosure of
Lewes's treachery, and the consequent resolue of the rebel English
Lords to turn again to John, Holinshed gives what follows, under
the year 1216, vol. iii. p. 193, col. 2, l. 6 :—

'About the same time, or rather in the yeare last past
as some hold, it fortuned that the vicount of Melune a
French man, fell sicke at London, and perceiuing that *Matth.*
death was at hand, he called vnto him certeine of the *Paris.*
English barons, which remained in the citie, vpon safe-
gard thereof, and to them made this protestation : "I The vicount
lament (saith he) your destruction and desolation at hand, discouereth
bicause ye are ignorant of the perils hanging ouer your the purpose
heads.   For this vnderstand, that Lewes, and with him of Lewes.
16 earles and barons of France, haue secretlie sworne
(if it shall fortune him to conquere this realme of England, & to be crowned king) that he will kill, banish, and [when vic-
confine all those of the English nobilitie (which now doo kill all his
serue vnder him, and persecute their owne king) as English
traitours and rebels, and furthermore will dispossesse all Nobles,]
their linage of such inheritances as they now hold in
England.   And bicause (saith he) you shall not haue
doubt hereof, I which lie here at the point of death, doo
now affirme vnto you, and take it on the perill of my
soule, that I am one of those sixteen that haue sworne
to performe this thing : wherefore I aduise you to prouide
for your owne safeties, and your realmes which you now
destroie, and keepe this thing secret which I haue vttered
vnto you."   After this speech was vttered he streightwaies The vicount
died. of Melune
dieth.

'When these words of the lord of Melune were opened
vnto the barons, they were, and not without cause, in
great doubt of themselues, for they saw how Lewes had
alredie placed and set Frenchmen in most of such

castels and townes as he had gotten, the right whereof
indeed belonged to them. And againe, it greeued them
much to vnderstand, how besides the hatred of their
prince, they were euerie sundaie and holiedaie openlie
accursed in euerie church, so that manie of them inwardlie
relented, and could haue bin contented to haue returned
to king Iohn, if they had thought that they should thank-
fullie haue beene receiued.'

The English nobilitie beginneth to mislike of the match which they had made with Lewes.

For Scene vi, Pt. II, p. 28-32,—John's arrival at Swinstead
Abbey, after the loss of his troops in the Wash—and for his death
in Sc. viii, p. 35-8, the following is in *Holinshed*, iii. 194, col. 1, l.
45. (Of the several reported causes of John's death, the Playwright
took the first.)

'Thus the countrie being wasted on each hand, the
king hasted forward till he came to Wellestreme sands,
where passing the washes he lost a great part of his
armie, with horsses and carriages, so that it was iudged
to be a punishment appointed by God, that the spoile
which had beene gotten and taken out of churches,
abbeies, and other religious houses, should perish, and
be lost by such means togither with the spoilers. Yet
the king himselfe, and a few other, escaped the violence
of the waters, by following a good guide. But as some
haue written, he tooke such greefe for the losse susteined
at this passage, that immediatelie therevpon he fell into
an ague, the force and heat whereof, togither with his
immoderate feeding on rawe peaches, and drinking of
new sider, so increased his sickenesse, that he was not
able to ride, but was faine to be carried in a litter pre-
sentlie made of twigs, with a couch of strawe vnder him,
without any bed or pillow, thinking to haue gone to
Lincolne, but the disease still so raged and grew vpon
him, that he was inforced to staie one night at the castell
of Laford, and on the next day with great paine, caused
himselfe to be caried vnto Newarke, where in the castell
through anguish of mind, rather than through force of
sicknesse, he departed this life the night before the nineteenth day of October, in the yeare of his age fiftie and
one, and after he had reigned seauenteene yeares, six
moneths, and seauen and twentie daies.

The losse of the kings carriages.

Matth. Paris. Matth. West.

King Iohn falleth sicke of an ague. Matth. Paris.

Laford. Matth. West. Matt. Paris.

King Iohn departed this life.

'¶ There be which haue written, that after he had lost
his armie, he came to the abbeie of Swineshead in Lin-
colneshire, and there vnderstanding the cheapenesse and
plentie of corne, shewed himselfe greatlie displeased there-
with, as he that for the hatred which he bare to the English

[r. Some say that

¹ p. 194, col. 2.

people, that had so traitorouslie reuolted from him vnto his aduersarie Lewes, wished all miserie to light vpon them, and therevpon said in his anger, that he would cause all kind of graine to be at a farre higher price, yer manie daies should passe. Wherevpon a moonke that heard him speake such words, being mooued with zeale for the oppression of his countrie, gaue the king poison in a cup of ale, wherof he first tooke the assaie, to cause the king not to suspect the matter, and so they both died in manner at one time.

[a Monk of Swinestead gave John poisoned ale, in revenge.] *Caxton.*

'There are that write, how one of his owne seruants did conspire with a conuert[1] of that abbeie, and that they prepared a dish of peares, which they poisoned, three of the whole number excepted, which dish the said conuert presented vnto him. And when the king suspected them to be poisoned indeed, by reason that such pretious stones as he had about him, cast foorth a certeine sweat, as it were bewraieng the poison, he compelled the said conuert to tast and eat some of them, who knowing the three peares which were not poisoned, tooke and eat those three, which when the king had seene, he could no longer absteine, but fell to, and eating greedilie of the rest, died the same night, no hurt happening to the conuert, who thorough helpe of such as bare no good will to the K. found shift to escape, and conueied himselfe awaie from danger of receiuing due punishment for so wicked a deed.

Gisburn & alij

[2. Others say that John eat poisond pears.]

'Beside these reports which yee haue heard, there are other that write, how he died of surfeting in the night, as Rafe Niger; some, of a bloudie flix,[2] as one saith that writeth an addition vnto Roger Houedon. And Rafe Cogheshall saith, that comming to Lin, (where he appointed Saueric de Mauleon to be capteine, and to take order for the fortifieng of that towne) he tooke a surfet there of immoderat diet, and withall fell into a laske, and after his laske had left him, at his comming to Laford in Lindsey, he was let bloud: furthermore to increase his other greefes and sorrowes for the losse of his carriage, iewels and men, in passing ouer the washes, which troubled him sore; there came vnto him messengers from Hubert de Burgh, and Gerard de Sotegam capteins of Douer castell, aduertising him, that they were not able to resist the forceable assalts and engins of the enimies, if speedie succour came not to them in due time. Whereat his greefe of mind being doubled, so as he might seeme euen oppressed with sorrow, the same increased his disease

The variable reports of writers, concerning the death of king Iohn.

[3. Others, that he died of a surfeit, and loss of bloud by flux and bleeding,

[with grief at his loss in the Wash, &c.]

Bernewell.

---

[1] A lay brother. See note, p. xxxix.   [2] dysentery.

so vehementlie, that within a small time it made an end
of his life (as before yee haue heard.)

'The men of warre that serued vnder his ensignes,
being for the more part hired souldiers and strangers,
came togither, and marching foorth with his bodie, each
man with his armour on his backe, in warlike order, conueied it vnto Worcester, where he was pompouslie buried
in the cathedral church before the high altar,[1] not for that
he had so appointed (as some write) but bicause it was
thought to be a place of most suretie for the lords and
other of his freends there to assemble, and to take order
in their businesse now after his deceasse. And bicause
he was somewhat fat and corpulent, his bowels were
taken out of his bodie, and buried at Croxton abbeie, a
house of moonks of the order called *Præmonstratenses*, in
Staffordshire, the abbat of which house was his physician.

'¶ How soeuer or where soeuer or when soeuer he
died, it is not a matter of such moment that it should
[2]impeach the credit of the storie: but certeine it is that
he came to his end, let it be by a surfet, or by other
meanes ordeined for the shortening of his life. The
manner is not so materiall as the truth is certeine. And
surelie, he might be thought to have procured against
himselfe manie molestations, manie anguishes & vexa-
ations, which nipt his hart & gnawd his very bowels with
manie a sore symptome or passion: all which he might
haue withstood if fortune had beene so fauourable, that
the loialtie of his subiects had remained towards him inuiolable, that his Nobles with multitudes of adherents had
not with such shamefull apostasie withstood him in open
fight, that forren force had not weakened his dominion, or
rather robbed him of a maine branch of his regiment,
that he himselfe had not sought with the spoile of his
owne people to please the imaginations of his ill affected
mind; that courtiers & commoners had with one assent
performed in dutie no lesse than they pretended in veritie,
to the preseruation of the state and the securitie of their
souereigne: all which presupposed plagues concurring,
what happinesse could the king arrogate to himselfe by
his imperiall title, which was through his owne default so
imbezelled, that a small remanent became his in right,
when by open hostilitie and accurssed papasie the greater
portion was pluckt out of his hands.

'Here therefore we see the issue of domesticall or
homebred broiles, the fruits of variance, the gaine that

[Burial of
John's body
in Worcester
Cathedral,

[his bowels
being interrd
at Croxton
Abbey.]

[He bred
troubles for
himself:

[his Nobles
rebeld
against him;

[he misspent
what he
wrung from
his people,

[and the
accursed

Papaey had
most of his
royalty.]

[All John's
and Eng-
land's ills

[1] *Tr. R.*, Pt. II, Sc. ix, l. 38-9, p. 40.   [2] p. 195, col. 1.

riseth of dissention, whereas no greater nor safer fortifica- [arose from
tion can betide a land, than when the inhabitants are all homebred
alike minded.   By concord manie an hard enterprise (in broils.]
common sense thought vnpossible) is atchiued, manie   See Part II
weake things become so defended, that without manifold *Tr. Raigne,*
force they cannot be dissolued.   From diuision and ix. 45·6, 53·4,
mutinies doo issue (as out of the Troiane horsse) ruines p. 40.]
of roialties, and decaies of communalties.'

   The presence of young Prince Henry (or K. Henry III.) in Sc.
viii, l. 127 is due to the old Playwright, for the boy was but 9 years
old at his father John's death, says Holinshed, iii. 197, col. 1 :—

   ' Henrie, the third of that name, the eldest sonne of K.
Iohn, a child of the age of nine yeres, began his reigne
ouer the realme of England the nineteenth day of October, *Anno Reg.* 1.
in the yeare of our Lord 1216, in the seuenth yeare of the   1216
emperour Frederike the second, and in the 36 yeare of
the reigne of Philip the second king of France.'

   For the end of Sc. vii, Pt. II, p. 38-9, the reported advance of
the French army against the English finds very little support in
Holinshed, iii. 200, col. 2, l. 64, under the year 1217 :—

   'On the other part, Lewes, who all this season remained [A.D. 1217.]
at London, being sore dismaied for the losse of his people,
began to feare euerie daie more and more, least by some
practise he should be betraied and deliuered into his
enimies hands.   Therefore he went about to make him- Lewes
selfe as strong as was possible, & fortifieng the citie, sent his father
messengers into France, to require his father to send him for aid.
more aid.   His father sorie to heare of his sons distresse,
and loth that he should take the foile, caused his daughter
the wife of Lewes, to prepare a power of men, that the
same might passe with all speed ouer into England to the
aid of hir husband.   For the French king himselfe would
not seeme to aid his sonne, bicause he was excommunicated : but his daughter in law, hauing licence and An armie
commission thereto, gat togither three hundred knights, prepared in
or men of armes, whome with a great number of other come to the
souldiers and armed men, she sent downe to Caleis, succour of
where Eustace the monke had prouided a nauie of ships Lewes.
to conueie them ouer into England.   But how they sped
you shall heare anon.
   ' In the meane time the earle of Pembroke approched *Polydor.*
towards London, purposing to assaile the citie now in
this opportunitie of time, letting passe no occasion that
might further his proceedings, night and day studieng

how to recouer the realme wholie out of the Frenchmens hands, and to set the same at libertie: so that what was to be deuised, he did deuise, and what was to be doone, that he did, not forslowing anie occasion or opportunitie that might be offered. The English barons also calling to mind the benefit which they had receiued at the Frenchmens hands in time of their most need, sought now by all means possible, some waie how to procure a peace betwixt king Henrie and the said Lewes, thinking by that means to benefit themselues, and to gratifie him in lieu of his former courtesie bountifullie shewed in a case of extremitie, which bicause it was obteined in a wished time was the more acceptable, whereas being lingered it had beene the lesse welcome, as one saith,

Gratia quæ tarda est ingrata est, gratia namque
Quùm fieri properat, gratia grata magis.

' Herevpon they caused dailie new articles of agreement to be presented in writing vpon the said Lewes, as from king Henrie. But while these things were a dooing, the earle of Penbroke and other the lords that tooke part with king Henrie, hauing aduertisement that a new supplie of men was readie to come and aid Lewes, they appointed Philip de Albenie and Iohn Marshall to associat with them the power of the cinque ports, and to watch for the comming of the aduersaries, that they might keepe them from landing, who on saint Bartholomews day set forth from Caleis, in purpose to arriue in the Thames, and so to come vp the riuer to London. Howbeit Hubert de Burgh capiteine of the castell of Douer, togither with the said Philip de Albenie and Iohn Marshall, with other such power as they could get togither of the cinque ports, hauing not yet aboue the number of 40 ships great & small, vpon the discouering of the French fleet, which consisted of 80 great ships, besides other lesser vessels well appointed and trimmed, made foorth to the sea. And first coasting aloofe from them, till they had got the wind on their backs, came finallie with their maine force to assaile the Frenchmen, and with helpe of their crossebowes and archers at the first ioining, made great slaughter of their enimies, and so grapling togither, in the end the Englishmen bare themselues so manfullie, that they vanquished the whole French fleet, and obteined a famous victorie.'

For Sc. ix of Part II (p. 39), the Dolphin's agreement with Henry to quit England, Holinshed says, under 1217 (vol. iii. p. 201, col. 2, l. 8):—

Side notes:

The diligence of the earle of Penbroke.

[The Barons seek to make peace betweene K. Henry and the Dolphin.]

Auson in epig.

Matth. Paris.

[Watch kept against the fresh French soldiers and fleet.]

Hubert de Burgh assaileth the French fleet.

The French fleet is vanquished.

'But Lewes, after he vnderstood of this mischance[1]
happening to his people that came to his aid, began not
a litle to despaire of all other succour to come vnto him
at any time heerafter: wherfore he inclined the sooner
vnto peace; so that at length he tooke such offers of
agreement as were put vnto him, and receiued furthermore a sum of monie for the release of such hostages as
he had in his hands, togither with the title of the king- An accord betwixt K. Henrie & Lewes.
dome of England, and the possession of all such castels
and holds as he held within the realme. ¶ The French The English chronicle saith a thousand pounds.
chronicle (to the which the chronicle of Dunstable and
Matthew Paris doo also agree) affirmeth that he receiued
fifteene thousand marks. Moreouer, the popes legat absolued Lewes, and all those that had taken his part in the
offense of disobedience shewed in attempting the warre *Matth. Paris.*
against the popes commandement.

'Then Lewes, with all his complices that had bin
excommunicated, sware vpon the holie euangelist, that
they should stand to the iudgement of holie church, and
from thenceefoorth be faithfull vnto the pope and to the [Lewes sweats that he'll leave England.]
church of Rome. Moreouer, that he with his people
should incontinentlie depart out of the realme, and neuer
vpon euill intent returne againe. And that so farre as
in him laie, he should procure his father king Philip, to
make restitution vnto king Henrie of all the right which
he had in the parts beyond the sea: and that when he
should be king of France, he should resigne the same in
most quiet manner.

'On the other part, king Henrie tooke his oth, togither
with the legat, and the earle of Penbroke gouernour of
the realme, that he should restore vnto the barons of his [Henry swears to restore his subjects their liberties.]
realme, and to other his subiects, all their rights and
heritages, with all the liberties before demanded, for the
which the discord was mooued betwixt the late king Iohn
and his barons. Moreouer, all prisoners on both parts
were released and set at libertie, without paieng anie
ransome: yea, and those which had couenanted to paie,
and vpon the same were set at libertie before the conclusion of this peace, were now discharged of all summes
of monie which then remained vnpaid.

'This peace was concluded on the eleuenth day of [Peace concluded on Sept. 11, 1217, at
September, not farre from Stanes, hard by the riuer of
Thames, where Lewes himselfe, the legat Guallo, and

---

[1] The loss of the French fleet and men sent to him, not, as the Play
says, on the Goodwin Sands (Pt. II, sc. vii, l. 33, p. 337), but by
the victory of the English ships, page xxxiv, above.

diuerse of the spiritualtie, with the earle of Penbroke lord
gouernor of the realme, and others, did meet and talke
about this accord. Now when all things were ordered
and finished agreeable to the articles and couenants of
the peace, so farre as the time present required, the lords
of the realme (when Lewes should depart homeward)
attended him to Douer in honorable wise, as apperteined,
and there tooke leaue of him, and so he departed out of
the realme about the feast of saint Michaell.'

Of K. John's person and character, Holinshed, besides the
extract on p. xxxii, &c., says (*Hol.* iii. 196/2, l. 4) :—

'He was comelie of stature,[1] but of looke and countenance displeasant and angrie, somewhat cruell of nature,
as by the writers of his time he is noted, and not so
hardie as doubtfull[2] in time of perill and danger. But
this seemeth to be an enuious report vttered by those
that were giuen to speake no good of him whome they
inwardlie hated.'

(*Hol.* iii. 196/1, col. 67.) 'Moreouer, the pride and pretended authoritie of the cleargie he could not well abide,
when they went about to wrest out of his hands the prerogatiue of his princelie rule and gouernment. True it is that
to mainteine his warres which he was forced to take in
hand, as well in France as elsewhere, he was constreined
to make all the shift he could deuise to recouer monie; and
bicause he pinched their pursses, they conceiued no small
hatred against him, which when he perceiued, and wanted
peraduenture discretion to passe it ouer, he discouered now
and then in his rage his immoderate displeasure, as one
not able to bridle his affections, a thing verie hard in a
stout stomach, and thereby missed now and then to compasse that which otherwise he might verie well haue
brought to passe.'

The old Playwright's treatment of his Material.—If Shakspere
had not rewritten *The Troublesome Raigne*, I think the Author
of it would have got more credit for his work than he has yet
obtained. As the case stands, almost all the Shakspere critics
—save Mr. W. Watkiss Lloyd in his *Critical Essays on Shakespeare*,
[1856], ed. 1875, p. 195-6, &c.—have felt bound to run down the old
Playwright and run up Shakspere. They don't seem to have askt them-
selves what merit Shakspere saw in the old play, that he was content
to write his own *King John* on his foregoer's lines (more or less), and
go no further than the *T. R.* for his material. They do not give the

[1] But 'fat and corpulent' at last, p. xxxii, above.   [2] hesitating, afraid.

Playwright credit for having recognized before Shakspere, that—in Elizabethan days at least—comedy had to be mixt with history in order to get an effective historical play. They forget that if Shakspere had his first lesson of the kind in *The Contention* and *2 Henry VI*, it made so little impression upon him that after it he wrote *Richard II.* and *Richard III.* without comic relief—and made his gardeners in the former play talk like philosophers—while after the *Troublesome Raigne* and *King John*, he learnt to put Falstaffe and comedy into *Henry IV.* and *V.*[1] They pass over the fact that Shakspere put his seal of approval on the old Playwright's invention of Falconbridge and his mother, &c., his alteration of Holinshed's characters of Arthur, of Limoges, &c., and his avoidance of Constance's re-marriages. They do not give the earlier dramatist credit for his keeping clear of one great blemish in Shakspere's play, the non-showing of the motive for the poisoning of John by the Swinstead monk. They are not as fair to the old Playwright as Shakspere himself was. He evidently said to himself when he saw (or perchance read the MS. of) the *Troublesome Raigne:* 'this play has merit; it 'll do for me; I can make a better thing of it; but the man who wrote it is no fool: he's given me all the material I want, and hints that I can develop; and I thank him for them.'

Though it is quite true that no good play can be made of the historic John, who degraded himself from the representative of England's independence into the Pope's tool, from a man into a cur, yet it is clear that the old Playwright made a very fair drama on the subject for his time. That Scene xi. of Part 1, p. 41-2, when the Bastard finds the Nun lockt up in the Prior's chest "To hide her from lay men," and then discovers 'Friar Lawrence' lockt up in the ancient Nun's chest, must have been a very telling one on the Elizabethan stage: you can fancy the audience's chuckles over it. So also must the Falconbridge incident, I. i. p. 7-17, and the Bastard killing Limoges on the stage, Pt. I, sc. xi, p. 35, have been thoroughly appreciated. Besides these scenes, the pathos of Arthur's death, the patriotism of the resistance to the Pope, and to John's oppressive taxation, the treachery of the French turning the nobles back to their allegiance, the final echo of the Chronicler,

> "Let *England* liue but true within it selfe,
> And all the world can neuer wrong her state. . . .
> If England's Peeres and people ioyne in one,
> Nor Pope, nor *France*, nor *Spaine* can doo them wrong,"—

all these points must have appeald strongly to an audience of Elizabeth's time, to whom home strife, Armada threats, disputed succession to the throne, and Papal intrigues, were matters of life-long familiarity.

---

[1] 'Post hoc, sed non propter hoc' is the answer. All I contend for is, that the *Tr. R.* may have been one of the many causes of the result.

The freedom with which the old Playwright used his Chronicle material must strike every one who reads or skims over these Forewords. And altogether, many as are the blemishes of *The Troublesome Raigne*, no fair-minded reader will deny or belittle its merits. ;

I ought perhaps to mention that—following earlier suggestions of possible authorship, he says—Mr. Fleay has turned the old Playwright into three, Greene, Peele, and Lodge, and has assignd to each the part of the Play he is supposed to have written (*K. John*, Collins, 1878, p. 33-5). To these suggestions and the statements in support of them, I attach no value myself; but other readers may do so. Minds differ. To Mr. Fleay's claim that "the original plot was laid down for the early play by Shakespeare" (*ib.* p. 11)—less the Friar and Nun scene (p. 25)—I cannot conceive many reasonable beings agreeing. But thought is free. After the acceptance of the Baconian and Dónnelly hypotheses by some creatures bearing the form of men and women, anything is possible.[1]

I have now only to thank my friend, Mr. W. G. Stone, for his help, and to ask every owner of a copy of this volume to make in the last pages of the Text, the corrections noted below.

British Museum, under the electric light,
    20 Nov. 1888, 7.45 p.m.

[1] As to Mr. Fleay's mention, on his p. 22, of Mr. Daniel adopting his Table prefixed to Marlowe's *Edw. II*, I note that Mr. Daniel made his Table showing the difference between the Qo. and Fo. of *Henry V.* (Parallel Text, N. Sh. Soc.) quite independently of Mr. Fleay's table showing how the actors' parts in *E two. II.* might be doubled. The object of the two Tables was altogether different, tho' the result of Mr. Daniel's—unconsciously to him—was that a reader could tell from it how to double certain parts.
   The foregoing extracts from Holinshed were of course made by Mr. Stone and myself without reference to Mr. Fleay's in his edition of *King John*.

By some oversight or accident, the corrected proof of sheet E which I returnd to Mr. Praetorius, was not sent to Hamburg, so that the following Corrections have to be made in the text :—

p. 34, Sc. vii, l. 41, word 3 is 'fled'; l. 46, word 8 is 'Nauies'
p. 34, Sc. viii, l. 18, syllable 1 is 'tie'; word 7 'surfet'
p. 35, l. 40, word 3 is 'so'
p. 36, l. 59, word 2 is 'fierce'; l. 75, word 3 is 'forgiue'
p. 37, l. 98, word 1 is 'But'; l. 102, word 2 is 'roote'; l. 120, there is no stop after 'fee'
p. 38, l. 150, word 4 is 'defiance' (alterd in Hamburg to 'destance')
p. 39, Sc. ix, l. 5, last word is 'lyes'
p. 39, Sc. ix, l. 11, word 4 is 'chiefest'

Part I, p. 8. *Falconbridge*. The name occurs several times in Holinshed. One owner of it was a contemporary of Edw. IV. ab. 1470. Mr. Watkiss Lloyd (*Essays on Shakespeare*, [1856] 1875, p. 196) suggests that some of Falconbridge's characteristics were got from that *raptarius nequissimus* and bastard, Falco de Brenta,—or Foukes de Brent, as Holinshed calls him,—who, though he was one of the Barons who wrested Magna Charta from King John (*Hol*. iii, 186/1, l. 38), yet gave him great help in his fight with his barons, and backt his son against Lewes. Holinshed tells of Foukes's deeds for John in 1215—16, on p. 189, col. 2, how he helpt in garrisoning the 'castell of Windsore, Hertford and Barkhamsted,' in wasting 'the counties of Essex and Hertford, Middlesex, Cambridge, Huntington,' subduing the towns, destroying the possessions of the barons, and setting fire to the suburbs of London. On Dec. 18, Foukes took 'the castell of Hanslap,' and Bedford, 'both the town and castell.'

'Vnto whom K. Iohn gaue not onlie that castell, but also committed to his keeping the castels of Northampton, Oxford and Cambridge. [*side: Castels deliuered to the keeping of Foukes de Brent.*]

'The king had this Foukes in great estimation, and amongst other waies to aduance him, he gaue to him in marriage, Margaret de Riuers, a ladie of high nobilitie, with all the lands and possessions that to her belonged.' *Hol*. iii. 189, 2, l. 47-55. [*side: Foukes de Brent aduanced by marriage.*]

In Henry III's time (1217), the castle of Hertford was surrenderd by Foukes's servant to Lewes, after a long defence (*Hol*. iii. 198/1); but on Feb. 22, 1218, Foukes spoild the town and abbey of St. Albans, as he had wasted all the towns and villages on his way thither from Hertford (*Hol*. iii. 199/1). Then he took part in the siege of 'Mountsorell beside Loughborough in Leicestershire' (*ib*.), and at the after siege of Lincoln, he made the attack which carried the city and castle, and which determind Lewes to come to terms with Henry III. The Earl of Pembrook turnd from his assault on Lincoln Castle, to attack the town gates. The French and their English allies followd to defend the town, leaving the castle unguarded;

(*Hol*. iii. 200/1, l. 42.) 'Thus whiles they were occupied on both parts, Fouks de Brent entered into the castell by a posterne gate on the backeside, and a great number of souldiers with him; and rushing into the citie out of the castell, he began a fierce batell with the citizens within the citie: which, when the Frenchmen perceiued, by the noise and crie raised at their backs, they ran to the place where the skirmish was, dooing their best to beat backe the aforesaid Foukes de Brent with his companie. But in the meane time the Englishmen, under the leading of Saucrie de Mauleon . . . brake open the gates and entred the citie. Then the fight was sore increased and mainteined for a time with great furie: so that it was hard to iudge who should haue the better. But at length the Frenchmen and those English lords that were with them, being sore laid-at on ech side, began to retire towards the gates, and finallie to turne their backs, and so fled awaie: but being beset round about with the king's horssemen, they were straight waies either slaine or taken, for the most part of them.' l. 64. [*side: Fouks de Brent [gets thro' the Castle posterne, and fights in the City.] [Other Englishmen entred thro' the City gates.] The Frenchmen put to flight at Lincolne.*]

This manœuvre of Falco de Brenta—or Breauté: see *Annals of England*, 1876, p. 148, col. 2—may (as Mr. Watkiss Lloyd says) have suggested to Shakspere, Falconbridge's proposal that the English and French forces should attack Angiers from opposite sides, 'east and west,' *K. John*, II. i. 38.

---

p. xxxi, *convert*. 'Convert, *n*. 2. A lay friar, or brother, permitted to enter a monastery for the service of the house, but without orders, and not allowed to sing in the choir.'—Webster. Latin *conversus*: see D'Arnis.

THE CHARACTERS, IN THE ORDER OF THEIR
ONCOMING.

ARTHUR, Prince of Britaine, Sc. i, p. 5.

The Earl of PENBROOKE, Sc. i, p. 6; Sc. iii, p. 15; Sc. iv, p. 24; Sc. v, p. 26; Sc. viii, p. 38; Sc. ix, p. 39.

THOMAS PLANTAGINET, Earle of SALSBURIE, Sc. i, p. 6; Sc. iii, p. 15 (speaks, p. 18, 21); Sc. iv, p. 24; Sc. v, p. 26; Sc. viii, p. 38; Sc. ix, p. 39.

The Earl of ESSEX, Sc. i, p. 6; Sc. iii, p. 15; Sc. iv, p. 24; Sc. v, p. 26; Sc. viii, p. 38; Sc. ix, p. 39.

HUGHBERT, Sc. i, p. 7; p. 9.

King IOHN, Sc. ii, p. 8; Sc. iv, p. 24; Sc. vi, p. 28; Sc. viii, p. 34.

2 or 3 Nobles, Sc. ii, p. 8; Sc. iv, p. 24.

Peter, the *Prophet*, Sc. ii, p. 8.

The Bastard, Philip Faulconbridge (son of K. Richard I.), Sc. ii, p. 10; Sc. iii, p. 16; Sc. iv, p. 24; Sc. vi, p. 28; Sc. viii, p. 34; Sc. ix, p. 39.

Cardinal PANDULPH, Legate from the See of Rome, Sc. ii, p. 13; Sc. iv, p. 24; Sc. viii, p. 38; Sc. ix, p. 39.

A Messenger, Sc. ii, p. 15; Sc. iii, p. 19; Sc. iv, p. 24; Sc. vii, p. 33; Sc. viii, p. 37, 38.

The Earl of CHESTER, Sc. iii, p. 15; Sc. iv, p. 24; Sc. viii, p. 38; Sc. ix, p. 39.

The Earl BEAUCHAMPE, Sc. iii, p. 15; Sc. iv, p. 24; Sc. viii, p. 38; Sc. ix, p. 39.

The Earl of CLARE, Sc. iii, p. 15; Sc. iv, p. 24; Sc. viii, p. 38; Sc. ix, p. 39.

The Earl PERCY, Sc. iii, p. 15 (speaks, p. 19); Sc. iv, p. 24; Sc. viii, p. 38; Sc. ix, p. 39.

LEWES, the Dolphin of *France*, with his Troupe, Sc. iii, p. 20; Sc. iv, p. 24; (and his Armie,) Sc. vii, p. 32; Sc. ix, p. 39.

Earle BIGOT, Sc. iii, p. 20; Sc. iv, p. 24; Sc. viii, p. 38; Sc. ix, p. 39.

Vicount MELOUN, Sc. iii, p. 20 (speaks, p. 22); Sc. iv, p. 24; Sc. v, p. 26.

A French Lord, Sc. iii, p. 22; Sc. iv, p. 24.

2 English Lords, Sc. vi, p. 28.

The Abbot of *Swinsteed*, and certayne Monks, Sc. vi, p. 30; Sc. viii, p. 34.

The Monke who poisons K. John, Sc. vi, p. 31; Sc. viii, p. 36.

Another Messenger, Sc. vii, p. 33.

Another Messenger, Sc. vii, p. 33.

Two Friers, laying a Cloth, Sc. v.ii, p. 34.

Prince HENRY, afterwards King HENRY III of England, Sc. viii, p. 38; Sc. ix, p. 39.

THE
Second part of the

troublefome Raigne of King
Iohn, conteining *the death*
of Arthur Plantaginet,
the landing of Lewes, and
the poyfning of King
Iohn at Swinftead
Abbey.
As it was (fundry times) publikely aɛted by the
Queenes Maiefties Players, in the ho-
nourable Citie of
London.

Imprinted at London for *Sampfon Clarke.*
and are to be folde at his fhop, on the backe-
fide of the *Royall Exchange.*
1 5 9 1.

To the Gentlmen Readers.

THe changeles purpofe of determinde Fate
Gines period to our care,or harts content,
When heauens fixt time for this or that hath end :
Nor can earths pomp or pollicie preuent
The doome ordained in their fecret will.

    Gentles we left King Iohn repleate with bliffe
That Arthur liude,whom he fuppofed flaine;
And Hubert pofting to returne thofe Lords,
Who deemd him dead,and parted difcontent :
Arthur himfelfe begins our latter Act.
Our Act of outrage, defprate furie,death;
Wherein fond rafhnes murdreth firft a Prince,
And Monkifh fulfnes poyfneth laft a King.
Firft Scene fhews Arthurs death in infancie,
And laft concludes Iohns fatull tragedie.

A 2

*The second part of the troublesome Raigne
of King Iohn, containing the entraunce of Lewes
the French Kings sonne : with the poysoning of King
Iohn by a Monke.*

Enter yong *Arthur* on the walls.

Ow helpe good hap to further mine entent,
Crosse not my youth with any moe extreames :
I venter life to gaine my libertie,
And if I die, worlds troubles haue an end.
Feare gins disswade the strength of my resolue,
My holde will faile, and then alas I fall,
And if I fall, no question death is next :
Better desist, and liue in prison still.
Prison said I ? nay rather death than so :
Comfort and courage come againe to me.
Ile venter sure : tis but a leape for life.

He leapes, and brusing his bones, after he was from
his traunce, speakes thus ;

Hoe, who is nigh ? some bodie take me vp.
Where is my mother ? let me speake with her.
Who hurts me thus ? speake hoe, where are you gone ?
Ay me poore *Arthur*, I am here alone.
Why cald I mother, how did I forget ?
My fall, my fall, hath kilde my Mothers Sonne.
How will she weepe at tidings of my death ?
My death indeed, O God my bones are burst,

A 3   Sweete

Sweete Iesu saue my soule, forgiue my rash attempt.
Comfort my Mother, shield her from despaire,
When she shall heare my tragick ouerthrowe.
My heart controules the office of my toong,
My vitall powers forsake my brused trunck,
I ope I ope, heauen take my fleeting soule,
And Lady Mother all good hap to thee. He dyes.

Enter *Penbrooke, Salsburie, Essex.*

Essex My Lords of *Penbroke* and of *Salisbury*
We must be carefull in our pollicie
To vndermine the keyers of this place,
Else shall we neuer find the Princes graue.
   Penbrooke My Lord of *Essex* take no care for that,
I warrant you it was not closely done.
But who is this? lo Lords the withered flowre
Who in his life shinde like the Mornings blush,
Cast out a dowre, denide his buriall right,
A pray for birds and beasts to gorge vpon.
   Salsburie O ruthfull spectacle, O damned deede;
My sinnewes shake, my very heart doth bleede.
   Essex Leaue childish teares braue Lords of *England*,
If water-floods could fetch his life againe,
My eyes should conduit forth a sea of teares.
If sobbs would helpe, or sorrowes serue the turne,
My heart should volie out deepe piercing plaints,
But bootlesse wert to breath as many sighes
As might eclipse the brightest Somimers sunne,
Heere rests the helpe, a seruice to his ghost.
Let not the tyrant causer of this dole,
Liue to triumph in ruthfull massacres,
Giue hand and hart, and Englishmen to armes,
Tis Gods decree to wreake vs of these harmes,
   Penbrok The best aduise: But who commes posting heere.

Enter

Enter *Hughbert*.

Right noble Lords, I speake vnto you all,
The King intreates your soonest speed
To visit him, who on your present want,
Did ban and cursse his birth, himselfe and me.
For executing of his strict commaund.
I saw his passion, and at fittest time,
Assurde him of his cousins being safe,
Whome pittie would not let me doo to death;
He craues your company my Lords in haste,
To whome I will conduct young *Arthur* streight,
Who is in health vnder my custodie.

  Essex In health base villaine, wert not I leaue thy crime
To Gods reuenge, to whome reuenge belongs,
Heere shouldst thou perish on my Rapires point.
Callst thou this health? such health betide thy friends,
And all that are of thy condition.

  Hughbert My Lords, but heare me speake, & kil me then,
If heere I left not this yong Prince aliue,
Maugre the hasty Edict of the King,
Who gaue me charge to put out both his eyes,
That God that gaue me liuing to this howre,
Thunder reuenge vpon me in this place:
And as I tenderd him with earnest loue,
So God loue me, and then I shall be well.

Salis. Hence traptor hence thy councel is heerein. Exit *Hughb.*
Some in this place appoynted by the King
Haue throwne him from this lodging here aboue,
And sure the murther hath bin newly done,
For yet the body is not fully colde.

  Essex How say you Lords, shall we with speed dispatch.
Vnder our hands a packet into *Fraunce*
To bid the Dolphin enter with his force
To claime the Kingdome for his proper right,
His title maketh lawfull strength thereto.
Besides the Pope, on perill of his cursse,

                                     Hath

The troublesome Raigne

K. John
IV. iii.

Hath bard vs of obedience vnto *Iohn*,
This hatefull murder, *Lewes* his true discent,
The holy charge that wee receiue from *Rome*,
Are weightie reasons if you like my reede,
To make vs all perseuer in this deede.

   Pembrooke My Lord of *Essex*, well haue you aduisde,
I will accord to further you in this.

   Salsbury And *Salsbury* will not gainsay the same.
But aid that course as far foorth as he can.

   Essex Then each of vs send straight to his Allyes.
To winne them to this famous enterprise,
And let vs all yclad in Palmers weede,
The tenth of April at Saint *Edmonds Bury*
Meete to confer, and on the Altar there
Sweare secrecie and aid to this aduise.
Meane while let vs conueigh this body hence,
And giue him buriall as befits his state,
Keeping his months minde and his obsequies
With solemne intercession for his soule.
How say you Lordings, are you all agreed?

   Pembrooke The tenth of Aprill at Saint *Edmonds Bury*
God letting not, I will not faile the time.

   Essex Then let vs all conuey the body hence. Exeunt.

    Enter King *Iohn* with two or three and the Prophet.

                        (not in
                        K. John)

   Iohn Disturbed thoughts, foredoomers of mine ill,
Distracted passions, signes of growing harmes,
Strange Prophecies of imminent mishaps,
Confound my wits, and dull my senses so,
That euery obiect these mine eyes behold
Seeme instruments to bring me to my end.
Ascension day is come, *Iohn* feare not then
The prodigies this pratling Prophet threates.
Tis come indeede: oh were it fully past,
Then were I careles of a thousand feares,

                        The

of King Iohn.

The Diall tells me, it is twelue at noone.
Were twelue at midnight past, then might I vaunt
False seers prophecies of no import.
Could I as well with this right hand of mine
Remoue the Sunne from our Meridian,
Vnto the moonsted circle of thantipodes,
As turne this steele from twelue to twelue agen,
Then *Iohn* the date of fatall prophecies
Should with the Prophets life together end.
But *Multa cadunt inter calicem supremaque labre*.
Peter, vnsay thy foolish doting dreame,
And by the Crowne of *England* héere I sweare,
To make thee great, and greatest of thy kin.

   Peter King *Iohn*, although the time I haue prescribed
Be but twelue houres remayning yet behinde,
Yet do I know by inspiration,
Ere that fixt time be fully come about,
King *Iohn* shall not be King as heeretofore.

   Iohn Vain buzzard, what mischaunce can chaunce so soone,
To set a King beside his regall seate :
My heart is good, my body passing strong,
My land in peace, my enemies subdewd,
Only my Barons storme at *Arthurs* death,
But *Arthur* liues, I there the challenge growes,
Were he dispatcht vnto his longest home,
Then were the King secure of thousand foes.
Hubert what news with thée, where are my Lords?

   Hubert Hard newes my Lord, *Arthur* the louely Prince
Seeking to escape ouer the Castle walles,
Fell headlong downe, and in the cursed fall
He brake his bones, and there before the gate
Your Barons found him dead, and breathlesse quite.

   Iohn Is *Arthur* dead? then *Hubert* without more words
        hang the Prophet.
Away with *Peter*, villen out of my sight,
I am deafe, be gone, let him not speake a word,

           B   Now

Now *Iohn*, thy feares are vanisht into smoake,
Arthur is dead, thou guiltlesse of his death.
Sweete Youth, but that I striued for a Crowne,
I could haue well affoorded to thine age
Long life, and happines to thy content.

Enter the Bastard.

Iohn Philip, what newes with thee?
Bastard The newes I heard was *Peters* prayers,
Who wisht like fortune to befall vs all:
And with that word, the rope his latest friend,
Kept him from falling headlong to the ground.
Iohn There let him hang, and be the Rauens foode,
While *Iohn* triumphs in spight of Prophecies.
But whats the tidings from the Popelings now.
What say the Monkes and Priests to our proceedings?
Or wheres the Barons that so sodainly
Did leaue the King vpon a false surmise?
Bastard The Prelates storme & thirst for sharpe reuēge,
But please your Maiestie, were that the worst,
It little skild: a greater danger growes,
Which must be weeded out by carefull speede,
Or all is lost, for all is leueld at.
Iohn More frights and feares, what ere thy tidings be,
I am preparde: then *Philip* quickly say,
Meane they to murder, or imprison me,
To giue my crowne away to *Rome* or *Fraunce*;
Or will they each of them become a King?
Worse than I thinke it is, it cannot be.
Bastard Not worse my Lord, but euerie whit as bad.
The Nobles haue elected *Lewes* King,
In right of Ladie *Blanche* your Neece, his Wife:
His landing is expected euerie hower.
The Nobles, Commons, Clergie, all Estates,
Incited chiefely by the *Cardinall*,

Pandulph

(not in
K. John)

Pandulph that lius here Legate for the Pope,
Thinks long to see their new elected King.
And for vndoubted proofe, see here my Liege
Letters to me from your Nobilitie,
To be a partie in this action:
Who vnder show of fained holines,
Appoynt their meeting at *S.Edmonds Bury*,
There to consult, conspire, and conclude
The ouerthrow and downfall of your State.

John Why so it must be: one hower of content
Matcht with a month of passionate effects.
Why shines the Sunne to fauour this consort?
Why doo the windes not breake their brazen gates,
And scatter all these periurd complices,
With all their counsells and their damned drifts.
But see the welkin rolleth gently on,
Thcres not a lowring clowde to frowne on them;
The heauen, the earth, the sunne, the moone and all
Conspire with those confederates my decay.
Then hell for me if any power be there,
Forsake that place, and guide me step by step
To poyson, strangle, murder in their steps
These traitors: oh that name is too good for them,
And death is easie: is there nothing worse
To wreake me on this proud peace-breaking crew?
What saist thou *Philip*? why assists thou not,

Bastard These curses (good my Lord) fit not the season;
Help must descend from heauen against this treason?

John Nay thou wilt prooue a traitor with the rest,
Goe get thee to them, shame come to you all.

Bastard I would be loath to leaue your Highnes thus,
Yet you command, and I though grieud will goe.

John Ah *Philip* whether goest thou, come againe.

Bastard My Lord these motions are as passions of a mad (man.

John A mad man *Philip*, I am mad indeed,
My hart is mazd, my senses all foredone.

B 2   And

And *Iohn* of *England* now is quite vndone,
Was euer King as I oppꝛeſt with cares ?
Dame *Elianor* my noble Mother Quéene,
My onely hope and comfoꝛt in diſtreſſe,
Is dead, and *England* excommunicate,
And I am interdicted by the Pope,
All Churches curſt, their dooꝛes are ſealed vp,
And foꝛ the pleaſure of the Romiſh Pꝛieſt,
The ſeruice of the Higheſt is neglected,
The multitude (a beaſt of many heads)
Do with confuſion to their Soueraigne;
The Nobles blinded with ambitions fumes,
Aſſemble powers to beat mine Empire downe,
And moꝛe than this, elect a foꝛren King.
O *England*, wert thou euer miſerable,
King *Iohn* of *England* ſées thée miſerable :
Iohn, tis thy ſinnes that makes it miſerable,
Quicquid delirunt Reges, plectuntur Achiui.
Philip, as thou haſt euer loude thy King,
So ſhow it now : poſt to S. *Edmonds Bury*,
Diſſemble with the Nobles, know their dꝛiſts,
Confound their diueliſh plots, and damnd deuices,
Though *Iohn* be faultie, yet let ſubiects beare,
He will amend and right the peoples wꝛongs.
A Mother though ſhe were vnnaturall,
Is better than the kindeſt Stepdame is :
Let neuer Engliſhman truſt foꝛraine rule.
Then *Philip* ſhew thy fealtie to thy King.
And mongſt the Nobles plead thou foꝛ the King.
 Baſtard I goe my Loꝛd : ſée how he is diſtraught,
This is the curſed Pꝛieſt of *Italy*
Hath heapt theſe miſchiefes on this hapleſſe Land.
Now *Philip*, hadſt thou *Tullyes* eloquence,
Then mightſt thou hope to plead with good ſucceſſe. Exit.
 Iohn And art thou gone ? ſucceſſe may follow thee :
Thus haſt thou ſhewd thy kindnes to thy King.
                                        Sirra,

Sirra, in haſt goe greete the Cardinall,
Pandulph I meane, the Legate from the Pope.
Say that the King deſires to ſpeake with him.
Now *Iohn* bethinke thee how thou maiſt reſolue:
And if thou wilt continue *Englands* King,
Then caſt about to keepe thy Diadem;
For life and land, and all is leueld at.
The Pope of *Rome*, tis he that is the cauſe,
He curſeth thee, he ſets thy ſubiects free
From due obedience to their Soueraigne:
He animates the Nobles in their warres,
He giues away the Crowne to *Philips* Sonne,
And pardons all that ſeeke to murther thee:
And thus blinde zeale is ſtill predominant.
Then *Iohn* there is no way to keepe thy Crowne,
But ſinely to diſſemble with the Pope:
That hand that gaue the wound muſt giue the ſalue
To cure the hurt, els quite incurable.
Thy ſinnes are farre too great to be the man
T'aboliſh Pope, and Popery from thy Realme:
But in thy Seate, if I may geſſe at all,
A King ſhall raigne that ſhall ſuppreſſe them all.
Peace *Iohn*, here comes the Legate of the Pope,
Diſſemble thou, and whatſoere thou ſaiſt,
Yet with thy heart wiſh their confuſion.

Enter *Pandulph.*

Pand.   Now *Iohn*, vnworthie man to breath on earth,
That doſt oppugne againſt thy Mother Church:
Why am I ſent for to thy curſed ſelfe?
   Iohn   Thou man of God, Uicegerent for the Pope,
The holy Uicar of S. *Peters* Church,
Upon my knees, I pardon craue of thee,
And doo ſubmit me to the ſea of *Rome*,
And vow for penaunce of my high offence,

B 3   To

152

156

160

164

168

172

175

176

180

183

To take on me the holy Crosse of Chrift,
And carp Armes in holy Chriftian warres.

    Pandulph. No *Iohn,* thy crowching and diffembling thus
Cannot deceiue the Legate of the Pope,
Say what thou wilt, I will not credit thee :
Thy Crowne and Kingdome both are tane away,
And thou art curft without redemption.

    Iohn Accurft indæde to kneele to fuch a drudge,
And get no help with thy fubmiffion,
Unfheath thy fword, and fley the mifprowd Prieft
That thus triumphs ore thæ a mighty King :
No *Iohn* fubmit againe diffemble yet,
For Priefts and Women muft be flattered,
Yet holp Father thou thy felfe doft know
No time to late for finners to repent,
Abfolue me then, and *Iohn* doth fweare to do
The vttermoft what euer thou demaunoft.

    Pandulph Iohn, now I fee thy harty penitence,
I rew and pitty thy diftreft eftate,
One way is left to reconcile thy felfe,
And only one which I fhall fhew to thee.
Thou muft furrender to the fea of *Rome*
Thy Crowne and Diademe, then fhall the Pope
Defend thee from thinuation of thy foes.
And where his holineffe hath kindled *Fraunce,*
And fet thy fubiects hearts at warre with thee,
Then fhall he curffe thy foes, and beate them downe,
That feeke the difcontentment of the King.

    Iohn From bad to woorfe or I muft loofe my realme,
Or giue up Crowne for pennance vnto *Rome ?*
A miferie more piercing than the darts
That breake from burning exhalations power.
What : fhall I giue my Crowne with this right hand :
No : with this hand defend thy Crowne and thee.
What newes with thee.

                             Enter

(not in
K. Iohn)

Enter Messenger.

Please it your Maiestie, there is descried on the Coast of
 Kent an hundred Sayle of Ships, which of all men is
 thought to be the French Fleete, vnder the conduct of the
 Dolphin, so that it puts the Cuntrie in a mutinie, so they
 send to your Grace for succour.   220

K. Iohn How now Lord Cardinall, whats your best aduise,   224
These mutinies must be allayd in time
By pollicy or headstrong rage at least.
O Iohn, these troubles tyre thy wearyed soule,
And like to Luna in a sad Eclipse,   228
So are thy thoughts and passions for this newes.
Well may it be when Kings are grieued so,
The vulgar sort worke Princes ouerthrow.
  Cardinall K. Iohn, for not effecting of thy plighted vow,   232
This strange annoyance happens to thy land:
But yet be reconcild vnto the Church,
And nothing shall be grieuous to thy state.
  Iohn On Pandulph be it as thou hast decreed,   236
Iohn will not spurne against thy sound aduise,
Come lets away, and with thy helpe I trow
My Realme shall florish and my Crowne in peace.   239

Enter the Nobles, Penbrooke, Essex, Chester, Bewchampe,
Clare, with others.

Penbrooke Now sweet S. Edmond holy Saint in heauen,   1
Whose Shrine is sacred, high esteemd on earth,
Infuse a constant zeale in all our hearts
To prosecute this act of mickle waight,   4
Lord Bewchampe say, what friends haue you procurde,
  Bewchamp. The L. Fitz Water, L. Percy, and L. Rosse,
Uowd meeting heere this day the seuenth houre.
  Essex Under the cloke of holie Pilgrimage,   5

By

10

Sc. iii.　　　　The troublesome Raigne　　　　(not in
K. John)

9 　Bp that same houre on warrant of their faith,
　Phillip Plantagenet, a bird of swiftest wing,
　Lord *Euſtace*, *Veſey*, Lord *Creſſy*, and Lord *Mowbrey*,
12 　Appopnted meeting at S. *Edmonds* Shrine.
　　Pembroke Untill their preſence ile conceale my tale,
　Sweete complices in holie Chriſtian acts,
　That venture for the purchaſe of renowne,
16 　Thrice welcome to the league of high reſolue,
　That pawne their bodies for their ſoules regard.
　　Eſſex Now wanteth but the reſt to end this worke,
　In Pilgrims habit commes our holie troupe
20 　A furlong hence with ſwift vnwonted pace,
　May be they are the perſons you erſpect.　　　　　(zeale,
　　Pembroke With ſwift vnwonted gate, ſee what a thing is
　That ſpurts them on with feruence to this Shrine,
24 　Now iop come to them for their true intent
　And in good time heere come the warmen all
　That ſweate in body by the minds diſeaſe
　Hap and hartseaſe braue Lordings be your lot.
　　　　Enter the Baſtard *Phillip*. &c.
28 　Amen my Lords, the like betide your lucke,
　And all that trauaile in a Chriſtian cauſe.
　　Eſſex Cheerely replied braue braunch of kingly ſtock,
　A right *Plantaginet* ſhould reaſon ſo.
32 　But ſilence Lords, attend our commings cauſe,
　The ſeruile poke that payned vs with toyle,
　On ſtrong inſtinct hath fraind this conuentickle,
　To eaſe our necks of ſeruitudes contempt.
36 　Should I not name the foeman of our reſt,
　Which of you all ſo barraine in conceipt,
　As cannot leuell at the man I meane?
　But leaſt Enigmas ſhadow ſhining truth
40 　Plainely to paint as truth requires no arte.
　Theffect of this reſort importeth this,
　To roote and cleane extirpate tirant *Iohn*,
43 　Tirant I ſay, appealing to the man,

　　　　　　　　　　　　　　　　　　　　　　If

(not in
K. John)

If any heere that loues him, and I aske
What kindship, lenitie, oz chzistian raigne
Rules in the man, to barre this foule impeach.
First I inferre the *Chesters* bannishment:
Foz repzehending him in most vnchzistian crimes,
Was speciall notice of a tyzants will.
But were this all, the deuill should be saud,
But this the least of many thousand faults,
That circumstance with leisure might display.
Our pziuate wzongs, no parcell of my tale
Which now in pzesence, but foz some great cause
Might wish to him as to a moztall foe.
But shall I close the period with an acte
Abhozzing in the eares of Chzistian men,
His Cosens death, that sweet vnguilty childe,
Untimely butcherd by the tyzants meanes,
Heere is my pzofes as cleere as grauell bzooke,
And on the same I further must inferre,
That who vpholds a tyzant in his course,
Is culpable of all his damned guilt.
To show the which, is yet to be descrivd.
My Lozd of *Penbrooke* shew what is behinde,
Only I say that were there nothing else
To moue vs but the Popes most dzeadfull cursse,
Whereof we are assured if we fayle,
It were inough to instigate vs all
With earnestnesse of spzit to secke a meane
To dispossesse *Iohn* of his regiment.

    Penbrooke Well hath my Lozd of *Essex* tolde his tale,
Which I auer foz most substanciall truth,
And moze to make the matter to our minde,
I say that *Lewes* in chalenge of his wife,
Hath title of an vncontrouled plea
To all that longeth to our English Crowne,
Shozt tale to make, the Sea apostolick
Hath offerd dispensation foz the fault.

                      C   It

44

48

52

56

60

64

68

72

76

79

If any be, as trust me none I know
By planting *Lewes* in the Usurpers roome:
This is the cause of all our presence here,
That on the holie Altar we protest
To ayde the right of *Lewes* with goods and life,
Who on our knowledge is in Armes for *England.*
What say you Lords?
   Salsburie As *Pembrooke* sayth, affirmeth *Salsburie:*
Faire *Lewes* of *Fraunce* that spoused Lady *Blanch,*
Hath title of an vncontrouled strength
To *England,* and what longeth to the Crowne:
In right whereof, as we are true inform'd,
The Prince is marching hitherward in Armes.
Our purpose to conclude that with a word,
Is to inuest him as we may deuise,
King of our Countrey in the tyrants stead:
And so the warrant on the Altar sworne,
And so the intent for which we hither came.
   Bastard. My Lord of *Salsbury,* I cannot couch
My speeches with the needfull words of arte,
As doth beseeme in such a waightie worke,
But what my conscience and my dutie will
I purpose to impart.
For *Chesters* exile, blame his busie wit,
That medled where his dutie quite forbade:
For any priuate causes that you haue,
Me thinke they should not mount to such a height,
As to depose a King in their reuenge.
For *Arthurs* death King *Iohn* was innocent,
He desperat was the deathsman to himselfe,
With you to make a colour to your crime iniustly do impute
But where fell traptorisme hath residence,   (to his default,
There wants no words to set despight on worke.
I say tis shame, and worthy all reproofe,
To wrest such pettie wrongs in tearmes of right,
Against a King annoynted by the Lord.
                    Why

(not in
K. John)

Why *Salsburie* admit the wrongs are true,
Yet subiects may not take in hand reuenge,
And rob the heauens of their proper power,
Where sitteth he to whome reuenge belongs.
And doth a Pope, a Priest, a man of pride
Giue charters for the liues of lawfull Kings ?
What can he blesse, or who regards his curse,
But such as giue to man, and takes from God.
I speake it in the sight of God aboue,
Theres not a man that dyes in pour beliefe,
But sels his soule perpetually to payne.
And *Lewes*, leaue God, kill *Iohn*, please hell,
Make hauock of the welfare of your soules,
For heere I leaue you in the sight of heauen,
A troupe of traytors foode for hellish feends;
If you desist, then follow me as friends,
If not, then doo your worst as hatefull traytors.
For *Lewes* his right alas tis too too lame,
A senselesse clayme, if truth be titles friend.
In briefe, if this be cause of our resort,
Our Pilgrimage is to the Deuils Shrine.
I came not Lords to troup as traytors doo,
Nor will I counsaile in so bad a cause :
Please you returne, wee go againe as friends,
If not, I to my King, and you where traytors please. Exit.
  Percy A hote young man, and so my Lords procced,
I let him go, and better lost then found.
  Penbrooke What say you Lords, will all the rest procced,
Will you all with me sweare vpon the Aulter
That you wil to the death be ayd to *Lewes*, & enemy to *Iohn* ?
Euery man lay his hãd by mine, in witnes of his harts accord,
Well then, euery man to Armes to meete the King
Who is alreadie before *London*.

  Messenger Enter.

  Penbrooke What newes Harrold.

The

The right Chꝛiſtian Pꝛince my Maiſter, *Lewes* of *Fraunce*, is
at hand, comming to biſit pour Honoꝛs, directed hether by
the right honoꝛable *Richard* Carle of *Bigot*, to conferre
with pour Honoꝛs.

Penbrooke How nære is his Highneſſe,

Meſſenger Ready to enter your pꝛeſence.

    Enter *Lewes*, Earle *Bigot*, with his troupe.

Lewes Faire Loꝛds of *England*, *Lewes* ſalutes you all
As friends, and firme welwillers of his weale,
At whoſe requeſt from plenty flowing *Fraunce*
Croſſing the Ocean with a Southern gale,
He is in perſon come at your commaunds
To vndertake and gratifie withall
The fulneſſe of your fauours pꝛoffred him.
But woꝛlds bꝛaue men, omitting pꝛomiſes,
Till time be miniſter of moꝛe amends,
I muſt acquaint you with our foꝛtunes courſe.
The heauens dewing fauours on my head,
Haue in their conduct ſafe with victoꝛie,
Bꝛought me along your well manured bounds,
With ſmall repulſe, and little croſſe of chaunce.
Your Citie Rocheſter with great applauſe
By ſome deuine inſtinct layd armes aſide:
And from the hollow holes of *Thames*ſis
Eccho apace replide *Viue la roy*.
From thence, along the wanton rowling glade
To *Troynouant* your fayꝛe *Metropolis*,
With luck came *Lewes* to ſhew his troupes of *Fraunce*,
Wauing our Enſignes with the dallping windes,
The fearefull obiect of fell frowning warre;
Where after ſome aſſault, and ſmall defence,
Heauens map I ſay, and not my warlike troupe,
Temperd their hearts to take a friendly foe
Within the compaſſe of their high built walles,
Geuing me title as it ſeemd they wiſh.

                            Thus

(not in
K. John)

Thus Fortune (Lords) acts to pour forwardnes 184
Meanes of content in lieu of former griefe:
And may I liue but to requite you all,
Worlds wish were mine in dying noted yours.
  Salisbury Welcome the balme that closeth vp our wounds, 188
The soueraigne medcine for our quick recure,
The anchor of our hope, the onely prop,
Whereon depends our liues, our lands, our weale, 192
Without the which, as sheepe without their heard,
(Except a shepheard winking at the wolfe)
We stray, we pine, we run to thousand harmes.
No meruaile then though with vnwonted ioy,
We welcome him that beateth woes away. 196
  Lewes Thanks to you all of this religious league,
A holy knot of Catholique consent.
I cannot name you Lordings, man by man,
But like a stranger vnacquainted yet. 200
In generall I promise faithfull loue:
Lord *Bigot*, brought me to S. *Edmonds* Shrine,
Giuing me warrant of a Christian oath,
That this assembly came deuoted heere, 204
To sweare accord̄ing as your packets showd,
Homage and loyall seruice to our selfe,
I neede not doubt the suretie of your wills;
Since well I know for many of your sakes 208
The townes haue yeelded on their owne accords:
Yet for a fashion, not for misbeliefe,
My eyes must witnes, and these eares must heare
Your oath vpon the holy Altar sworne, 212
And after march to end our commings cause.
  Sals. That we intend no other then good truth,
All that are present of this holy League,
For confirmation of our better trust, 216
In presence of his Highnes sweare with me,
The sequel that my selfe shal vtter heere,

          C 3   *Thomas*

I *Thomas Plantaginet* Earle of *Salisbury*, sweare vpon the
Altar, and by the holy Armie of Saints, homage and alleag-
ance to the right Christian Prince *Lewes* of *Fraunce*, as true
and rightfull King to *England, Cornwall* and *Wales*, & to their
Territories, in the defence whereof I vppon the holy Altare
sweare all forwardnes.　　　　All the Eng. Lords sweare,

　　As the noble Earle hath sworne, so sweare we all.

Lewes I rest assured on your holy oath,
And on this Altar in like sort I sweare
Loue to you all, and Princely recompence
To guerdon your good wills vnto the full.
And since I am at this religious Shrine,
My good welwillers, giue vs leaue awhile
To vse some orisons our selues apart
To all the holy companie of heauen,
That they will smile vpon our purposes,
And bring them to a fortunate euent.

　　Salisbury　We leaue your Highnes to your good intent.
　　　　　　　　　　　　Exeunt Lords of *England*.

　　Lewes Now Vicount *Meloun*, what remaines behinde?
Trust me these traitors to their souereigne State
Are not to be belœude in any sort.

　　Meloun Indeed my Lord, they that infringe their oaths,
And play the rebells gainst their natiue King,
Will for as little cause reuolt from you,
If euer opportunitie incite them so:
For once forsworne, and neuer after sound,
Theres no affiance after periurie.

　　Lewes Well *Meloun* well, lets smooth with them awhile,
Vntill we haue asmuch as they can doo:
And when their vertue is exhaled drie,
Il hang them for the guerdon of their help,
Meane while wee'l vse them as a precious poyson
To vndertake the issue of our hope.

　　Fr. Lord Tis policie (my Lord) to bait our hookes
With merry smiles, and promise of much waight:

　　　　　　　　　　　　　　　　But

(not in
K. John)

But when your Highnes needeth them no moze.   254
Tis good make sure wozk with them, least indeede
They pzooue to you as to their naturall King.
   Melun Trust me my Lozd right well haue you aduisde   258
Tenpime foz vse, but neuer foz a spozt
Is to be dallped with, least it infect.
Were you instald, as soone I hope you shall:
Be free from traitozs, and dispatch them all.
   Lewes That so I meane, I sweare befoze you all   262
On this same Altar, and by heauens power,
Theres not an English traytoz of them all.
John ouce dispatcht, and I faire *Englands* King,
Shall on his shoulders beare his head one day,   266
But I will crop it foz their guilts desert:
Noz shall their heires enioy their Signozies,
But perish by their parents sowle amisse.
This haue I swozne, and this will I perfozme,   270
If ere I come vnto the height I hope.
Lay downe your hands, and sweare the same with mee.

      The French Lords sweare.

Why so, now call them in, and speake them faire,
A smile of *France* will feed an English foole.   274
Beare them in hand as friends, foz so they be:
But in the hart like traytozs as they are.

      Enter the English Lords.
Now famous followers, chieftaines of the wozld,
Haue we soillicited with heartie pzayer   278
The heauen in fauour of our high attempt.
Leaue we this place, and march we with our power
To rowse the Tyzant from his chiefest hold:
And when our labours haue a pzospzous end,   282
Each man shall reape the fruite of his desert.
And so resolude, bzaue followers let vs hence.
                   Enter   284

Enter K. *Iohn, Baſtard, Pandulph,* and a many prieſts
with them.

1 Thus *Iohn* thou art abſolude from all thy ſinnes,
And freed by oꝛder from our Fathers curſe.
Receiue thy Crowne againe, with this pꝛouiſo,
4 That thou remaine true liegeman to the Pope,
And carry armes in right of holy *Rome.*
  Iohn I holde the ſame as tenaunt to the Pope,
And thanke your Holines foꝛ your kindnes ſhowne.
8   *Philip* A pꝛoper ieſt, when Kings muſt ſtoop to Friers,
Neede hath no law, when Friers muſt be Kings.

Enter a Meſſenger.

10   *Meſſ.* Pleaſe it your Maieſtie, the Pꝛince of *Fraunce,*
With all the Nobles of your Graces Land,
Are marching hetherward in good aray.
Where ere they ſet their foote, all places yeeld :
14 Thy Land is theirs, and not a foote holds out
But *Douer* Caſtle, which is hard beſiegd.
  Pandulph Feare not King *Iohn,* thy kingdome is ý popes,
And they ſhall know his Holines hath power,
18 To beate them ſoone from whence he hath to doo.

Drums and Trumpets. Enter *Lewes, Melun, Salis-*
bury, Eſſex, Pembrooke, and all the Nobles from
Fraunce, and *England.*

19   *Lewes* *Pandulph,* as gaue his Holines in charge,
So hath the *Dolphin* muſtred vp his troupes
And wonne the greateſt part of all this Land,
But ill becomes your Grace Loꝛd Cardinall,
23 Thus to conuerſe with *Iohn* that is accurſt.

                              Pandulph

O

Pandulph *Lewes* of *France*, victozious Conqueroz,
Whoſe ſwozd hath made this Iſland quake foz fear ;
Thy foꝛwardnes to fight foꝛ holy *Rome*,
Shalbe remunerated to the full :
But know my Loꝛd, K. *John* is now abſolude,   28
The Pope is pleaſde, the Land is bleſt agen,
And thou haſt bzought eah thing to good effect.
It reſteth then that thou withdꝛaw thy powers,
And quietly returne to *Fraunce* againe :   32
Foꝛ all is done the Pope would wiſh thee doo.
     Lewes But als not done that *Lewes* came to doo.
Why *Pandulph*, hath K. *Philip* ſent his ſonne
And been at ſuch exceſſiue charge in warres,   36
Tobe diſmiſt with wozds ? K. *John* ſhall know,
England is mine, and he vſurps my right.
     Pand. *Lewes*, I charge thee and thy complices
Upon the paine of *Pandulphs* holy curſe,   40
That thou withdꝛaw thy powers to *Fraunce* againe,
And peeld vp *London* and the neighbour Townes
That thou haſt tane in *England* by the ſwozd.
     Melun Loꝛd Cardinall, by *Lewes* princely leaue, 44
It can be nought but vſurpation
In thee, the Pope, and all the Church of *Rome*,
Thus to inſult on Kings of Chꝛiſtendome,
Now with a wozd to make them carie armes,   48
Then with a wozd to make them leaue their armes.
This muſt not be : Pꝛince *Lewes* keepe thine owne,
Let Pope and Popelings curſe their bellyes full.
     Baſt. My Loꝛd of *Melun*, what title had the Pꝛince 52
To *England* and the Crowne of *Albion*,
But ſuch a title as the Pope confirmde :
The Pꝛelate now lets fall his fained claime :
Lewes is but the agent foꝛ the Pope,   56
Then muſt the *Dolphin* ceaſe, ſith he hath ceaſt :
But ceaſe oꝛ no, it greatly matters not,
If you my Loꝛds and Barrons of the Land   59

D   Will

Will leane the French, and cleaue vnto your King.
For shame ye Peeres of *England*, suffer not
Your selues, pour honours, and pour land to fall:
But with resolued thoughts beate back the French,
And free the Land from poke of seruitude.
   Salisbury *Philip*, not so, Lord *Lewes* is our King,
And we will follow him vnto the death.
   Pand. Then in the name of *Innocent* the Pope,
I curse the Prince and all that take his part,
And excommunicate the rebell Peeres
As traptors to the King, and to the Pope.
   Lewes Pandolph, our swords shall blesse our selues agen:
Prepare thee *Iohn*, Lords follow me pour King. *Exeunt.*
   Iohn Accursed *Iohn*, the diuell owes thée shame,
Resisting *Rome*, or peelding to the Pope, alls one.
The diuell take the Pope, the Peeres, and *Frannce:*
Shame be my share for peelding to the Priest.
   Pand. Comfort thy self K. *Iohn*, the Cardinall goes
Upon his curse to make them leaue their armes. *Exit.*
   Bastard Comfort my Lord, and curse the Cardinall,
Betake your self to armes, my troupes are prest
To answere *Lewes* with a lustie shocke:
The English Archers haue their quiuers full,
Their bowes are bent, the ppkes are prest to push:
God chære my Lord, K. *Richards* fortune hangs
Upon the plume of warlike *Philips* helme.
Then let them know his brother and his sonne
Are leaders of the Englishmen at armes.
   Iohn *Philip* I know not how to answere thee:
But let vs hence, to answere *Lewes* pride.

Excursions. Enter *Melonn* with English Lords.

   Mel. O I am slaine, Nobles, *Salisbury*, *Pembrooke*,
My soule is charged, heare me: for what I say
Concernes the Peeres of *England*, and their State.
                         Listen

Listen, braue Lords, a fearfull mourning tale   4
To be deliuered by a man of death.
Behold these scarres, the dole of bloudie *Mars*
Are harbingers from natures common foe,
Epting this trunke to *Tellus* prison house;   8
Lifes charter (Lordings) lasteth not an howre:
And fearfull thoughts, forerunners of my end,
Bids me giue Phisicke to a sickly soule.
O Peeres of *England*, know you what you doo,   12
Theres but a haire that sunders you from harme,
The hooke is bayted, and the traine is made,
And simply you runne doating to your deaths.
But least I dye, and leaue my tale vntolde,   16
With silence slaughtering so braue a crew,
This I auerre, if *Lewes* win the day,
Theres not an Englishman that lifts his hand
Against King *Iohn* to plant the heire of *Fraunce*,   20
But is already damnd to cruell death.
I heard it vowd; my selfe amongst the rest
Swore on the Altar aid to this Edict.
Two causes Lords, makes me display this drift,   24
The greatest for the freedome of my soule,
That longs to leaue this mansion free from guilt:
The other on a naturall instinct.
For that my Grandsire was an Englishman.   28
Misdoubt not Lords the truth of my discourse,
No frenzie, nor no braine sick idle fit,
But well aduisde, and wotting what I say,
Pronounce I here before the face of heauen,   32
That nothing is discouered but a truth.
Tis time to flie, submit your selues to *Iohn*,
The smiles of *Fraunce* shade in the frownes of death,
Lift up your swords, turne face against the French,   36
Expell the poke thats framed for your necks.
Back warmen, back, imbowell not the clyme.
Your seate, your nurse, your birth dayes breathing place,   39

D 2   That

The troublesome Raigne

That bred you, beares you, brought you vp in armes.
Ah be not so ingrate to digge your Mothers graue,
Preserue your lambes and beate away the Wolfe,
My soule hath said, contritions penitence
Layes hold on mans redemption for my sinne.
Farewell my Lords, witnes my faith when wee are met in
And for my kindnes giue me graue roome heere.   (heauen,
My soule doth fleete, worlds vanities farewell.

  Salf. Now ioy betide thy soule wel-meaning man,
How now my Lords, what cooling card is this,
A greater griefe growes now than earst hath been.
What counsell giue you, shall we stay and dye:
Or shall we home, and kneele vnto the King.

  Pemb. My hart misgaue this sad accursed newes:
What haue we done, fie Lords, what frenzie moued
Our hearts to yeeld vnto the pride of *Fraunce?*
If we perseuer, we are sure to dye:
If we desist, small hope againe of life.

  Salib. Beare hence the bodie of this wretched man,
That made vs wretched with his dying tale,
And stand not wayling on our present harmes,
As women wont: but seeke our harmes redresse.
As for my selfe, I will in hast be gon:
And kneele for pardon to our Souereigne *Iohn.*

  Pemb. I, theres the way, lets rather kneele to him,
Than to the French that would confound vs all, *Exeunt.*

        Enter *King Iohn carried betweene 2. Lords.*
  Iohn Set downe, set downe the load not worth your pain,
For done I am with deadly wounding griefe:
Sickly and succourles, hopeles of any good,
The world hath wearied me, and I haue wearied it:
It loaths I liue, I liue and loath my selfe.
Who pities me: to whom haue I been kinde:
But to a few; a few will pitie me.
  Why dye I not? Death scornes so vilde a pray.

                                    Why

Why liue I not, life hates so sad a prize.
I sue to both to be retapnd of either,
But both are deafe, I can be heard of neither.
Nor death nor life, yet life and neare the neere,
Ynirt with death biding I wot not where.

Philip. Now fares my Lord that he is tarped thus,
Not all the aukward fortunes yet befalne,
Made such impression of lament in me.
Nor euer did my eye attapnt my heart
With any obiect mouing more remorse,
Than now beholding of a mighty King,
Borne by his Lords in such distressed state.

John What news with thee, if bad, report it straite :
If good, be mute, it doth but flatter me.

Phillip Such as it is, and heauie though it be
To glut the world with tragick elegies,
Once will I breath to agrauate the rest.
Another moane to make the measure full.
The brauest bowman had not yet sent forth
Two arrowes from the quiuer at his side,
But that a rumor went throughout our Campe,
That Iohn was fled, the King had left the field.
At last the rumor scald these eares of mine,
Who rather chose as sacrifice for Mars,
Than ignominious scandall by retyre.
I cheerd the troupes as did the Prince of Troy
His weery followers gainst the Mirmidons,
Crying alowde S. George, the day is ours.
But feare had captiuated courage quite,
And like the Lamb before the greedie Wolfe,
So hartlesse fled our warmen from the feeld.
Short tale to make, my selfe amongst the rest,
Was faine to flie before the eager foe.
By this time night had shadowed all the earth,
With sable curteines of the blackest hue,
And senst vs from the fury of the French,

D. 3

9

12

16

20

24

28

32

36

40

44

As *Io* from the iealous *Iunos* eye,
When in the mozning our troupes did gather head,
Paſſing the waſhes with our carriages,
The impartiall tyde deadly and inexozable,
Came raging in with billowes threatning death,
And ſwallowed vp the moſt of all our men,
My ſelfe vpon a Galloway right frée, well paced,
Out ſtript the flouds that followed waue by waue,
I ſo eſcapt to tell this tragick tale.

Iohn Griefe vpon griefe, yet none ſo great a griefe,
To end this life, and thereby rid my griefe.
Was euer any ſo infortunate,
The right Idea of a curſſed man,
As I, pooze I, a triumph foz deſpight,
My feuer growes, what ague ſhakes me ſo:
How farre to Swinſteed, tell me do you know,
Preſent vnto the Abbot word of my repaire.
My ſickneſſe rages, to tirannize vpon me,
I cannot liue vnleſſe this feuer leaue me.

Phillip. Good cheare my Lozd, the Abbey is at hand,
Behold my Lozd the Churchmen come to meete you.

Enter the Abbot, and certayne Monks.

Abbot All health & happines to our ſoueraigne Lozd the
Iohn Noz health noz happines hath *Iohn* at all.　(King,
Say Abbot am I welcome to thy houſe.

Abbot Such welcome as our Abbey can afford,
Your Maieſty ſhalbe aſſured of.

Phillip The King thou ſeeſt is weake and very faint,
What viduals haſt thou to refreſh his Grace.

Abbot God ſtoze my Lozd, of that you neede not feare,
Foz Lincolneſhire, and theſe our Abbey grounds
Were neuer fatter, noz in better plight.

Iohn Phillip, thou neuer needſt to doubt of cates,
Noz King noz Lozd is ſeated halfe ſo well,
As are the Abbeys throughout all the land,
If any plot of ground do paſſe another,

The

The Friers fatten on it ſtreight :
But let vs in to taſte of their repaſt,
It goes againſt my heart to feed with them,
Or be beholding to ſuch Abbey groomes.   Exeunt.

    Manet the Monke.

  Monk. Is this the King that neuer loud a Frier :
Is this the man that doth contemne the Pope :
Is this the man that robd the holy Church,
And yet will flye vnto a Fryor :
Is this the King that aymes at Abbeys lands :
Is this the man whome all the world abhorres,
And yet will flye vnto a Fryor :
Accurſt be Swinſteed Abbey, Abbot, Friers,
Moncks, Nuns, and Clarks, and all that dwells therein,
If wicked *Iohn* eſcape aliue away.
Now if that thou wilt looke to merit heauen,
And be canonizd for a holy Saint :
To pleaſe the world with a deſeruing worke,
Be thou the man to ſet thy cuntrey free,
And murder him that ſeekes to murder thee.
    Enter the Abbot.
  Abbot Why are not you within to cheare the King :
He now begins to mend, and will to meate.
  Monk What if I ſay to ſtrangle him in his ſleepe :
  Abbot What at thy *mumpſimus?* away,
And ſeeke ſome meanes for to paſtime the King.
  Monk Ile ſet a dudgeon dagger at his heart,
And with a mallet knock him on the head.
  Abbot Alas, what meanes this Monke to murther me :
Dare lay my life heel kill me for my place,
  Monk Ile poyſon him, and it ſhall neare be knowne,
And then ſhall I be chiefeſt of my houſe.
  Abbot If I were dead, indeed he is the next,
But ile away, for why the Monke is mad,
And in his madneſſe he will murther me.
              Monk My

Monk My L. I cry your Lordship mercy, I saw you not.

Abbot Alas good *Thomas* do not murther me, and thou shalt haue my place with thousand thanks.

Monk I murther you, God sheeld from such a thought.

Abbot If thou wilt needes, yet let me say my prayers.

Monk I will not hurt your Lordship good my Lord: but if you please, I will impart a thing that shall be beneficiall to vs all.

Abbot Wilt thou not hurt me holy Monke, say on.

Monk You know my Lord the King is in our house,

Abbot True.

Monk You know likewise the King abhors a Frier,

Abbot True.

Monk And he that loues not a Frier is our enemy.

Abbot Thou sayst true.

Monk Then the King is our enemy.

Abbot True.

Monk Why then should we not kil our enemy, & the King being our enemy, why then should we not kill the King.

Abbot O blessed Monke, I see God moues thy minde to free this land from tyrants slauery.
But who dare venter for to do this deede?

Monk Who dare? why I my Lord dare do the deede,
Ile free my Countrey and the Church from foes,
And merit heauen by killing of a King.

Abbot *Thomas* kneele downe, and if thou art resolude,
I will absolue thee heere from all thy sinnes,
For why the deede is meritorious.
Forward and feare not man, for euery mouth,
Our Friers shall sing a Masse for *Thomas* soule.

Monk God and S. *Francis* prosper my attempt,
For now my Lord I goe about my worke.   Exeunt.

    Enter *Lewes* and his armie.

Lewes Thus victory in blouddy Lawrell clad,
Followes the fortune of young *Lodowicke*,
The Englishmen as daunted at our sight,

Fall

Fall as the fowle before the Eagles eyes,
Onely two crosses of contrary change
Do nip my heart, and vexe me with vnrest.
Lord *Melons* death, the one part of my soule,
A brauer man did neuer liue in *Fraunce*.
The other griefe, I thats a gall in deede,
To thinke that *Douer* Castell should hold out
Gainst all assaults, and rest impregnable.
Yee warlike race of *Francus Hectors* sonne,
Triumph in conquest of that tyrant *Iohn*,
The better halfe of *England* is our owne,
And towards the conquest of the other part,
We haue the face of all the English Lords,
What then remaines but ouerrun the land.
Be resolute my warlike followers,
And if good fortune serue as she begins,
The poorest peasant of the Realme of *Fraunce*
Shall be a maister ore an English Lord.

Enter a Messenger.

Lewes Fellow what newes.

Messen. Pleaseth your Grace, the Earle of *Salsbury*, *Pen-broke*, *Essex*, *Clare*, and *Arundell*, with all the Barons that did fight for thee, are on a suddeine fled with all their powers, to ioyne with *Iohn*, to driue thee back againe.

Enter another Messenger.

Messen. Lewes my Lord why standst thou in a maze,
Gather thy troups, hope out of help from *Fraunce*,
For all thy forces being fiftie sayle,
Conteyning twenty thousand souldyers,
With victuall and munition for the warre,
Putting from *Callis* in vnluckie time,
Did crosse the seas, and on the *Goodwin* sauds,
The men, munition, and the ships are lost.

Enter another Messenger.

Lewes More newes: say on.

Messen. Iohn (my Lord) with all his scattered troupes,

C   Flying

4

8

12

16

20

24

28

32

36

Flying the fury of your conquering sword,
As *Pharaoh* earst within the bloody sea,
So he and his enuironed with the tyde,
On *Lincolne* washes all were ouerwhelmed,
The Barons fled, our forces cast away.

Lewes Was euer heard such vnexpected newes :

Messenger Yet *Lodowike* reuiue thy dying heart,
King *Iohn* and all his forces are consumde,
The lesse thou needst the ayd of English Earles,
The lesse thou needst to grieue thy Names wracke,
And follow tymes aduantage with successe.

Lewes Braue *Frenchmen* armde with magnanimitie,
March after *Lewes* who will leade you on
To chase the Barons power that wants a head,
For *Iohn* is drownd, and I am *Englands* King.
Though our munition and our men be lost,
Phillip of *Fraunce* will send vs fresh supplyes. Exeunt.

Enter two Friers laying a Cloth.

Frier Dispatch, dispatch, the King desires to eate,
Would a might eate his last for the loue hee beares to
Churchmen.

Frier I am of thy minde to, and so it should be and we
might be our owne caruers.
I meruaile why they dine heere in the Orchard.

Frier I know not, nor I care not. The King coms.

Iohn Come on Lord Abbot, shall we sit together ?

Abbot Pleaseth your Grace sit downe.

Iohn Take your places sirs, no pomp in penury, all beg-
gers and friends may come, where necessitie keepes the
house, curtesie is bard the table, sit downe *Phillip*.

Bast. My Lord, I am loth to allude so much to ye prouerb
honors change maners : a King is a King, though fortune do
her worst, and we as dutifull in despight of her frowne, as if
your highnesse were now in the highest type of dignitie.

Iohn Come, no more ado, and you tell me much of dignitie, youle mar my appetite in a surfet of sorrow.

What

What cheere Lord Abbot, me thinks you frowne like an host
that knowes his guest hath no money to pay the reckoing?
 Abbot No my Liege, if I frowne at all, it is for I feare
this cheere too homely to entertaine so mighty a guest as
your Maiesty.
 Bastard I thinke rather my Lord Abbot you remember
my last being heere, when I went in progresse for powtches,
and the rancor of his heart breakes out in his countenance,
to shew he hath not forgot me.
 Abbot Not so my Lord, you, and the meanest follower
of his maiesty, are hartely welcome to me.
 Monke Wassell my Liege, and as a poore Monke may
say, welcome to Swinsted.
 Iohn Begin Monke, and report hereafter thou wast taster
to a King.
 Monk As much helth to your highnes, as to my own hart.
 Iohn I pledge thee kinde Monke.
 Monke The meriest draught þ euer was dronk in Englãd.
Am I not too bold with your Highnesse.
 Iohn Not a whit, all friends and fellowes for a time.
 Monke If the inwards of a Toad be a compound of any
proofe: why so it workes.
 Iohn Stay Phillip wheres the Monke?
 Bastard He is dead my Lord.
 Iohn Then drinke not Phillip for a world of wealth.
 Bast. What cheere my Liege, your cullor gins to change.
 Iohn So doth my life, O Phillip I am poysond.
The Monke, the Deuill, the poyson gins to rage,
It will depose my selfe a King from raigne.
 Bastard This Abbot hath an interest in this act.
At all aduentures take thou that from me.
There lye the Abbot, Abbey, Lubber, Deuill.
March with the Monke vnto the gates of hell.
How fares my Lord?
 Iohn Phillip some drinke, oh for the frozen Alps,
To tumble on and cwle this inward heate,
That rageth as the fornace seuenfold hote.

To burne the holy tree in *Babylon*,
Power after power forsake their proper power,
Only the hart impugnes with faint resist
The fierce inuade of him that conquers Kings,
Help God, O payne, ope *Iohn*, O plague
Inflicted on thee for thy grieuous sinnes.
Phillip a charge, and by and by a graue,
My legges disdaine the carriage of a King.
   Bastard. A good my Lege with patience conquer griefe,
And beare this paine with kingly fortitude.
   Iohn Me thinks I see a cattalogue of sinne
Wrote by a fiend in Marble characters,
The least enough to loose my part in heauen.
Me thinks the Deuill whispers in mine eares
And tels me tis in vayne to hope for grace,
I must be damnd for *Arthurs* sodaine death,
I see I see a thousand thousand men
Come to accuse me for my wrong on earth,
And there is none so mercifull a God
That will forgiue the number of my sinnes.
How haue I liud, but by anothers losse?
What haue I loud but wrack of others weale?
When haue I vowd, and not infringd mine oath?
Where haue I done a deede deseruing well?
How, what, when, and where, haue I bestowd a day
That tended not to some notorious ill.
My life repleat with rage and tyranis,
Craues little pittie for so strange a death.
Or who will say that *Iohn* disceasd to soone,
Who will not say he rather liud to long.
Dishonor did attaynt me in my life,
And shame attendeth *Iohn* vnto his death.
Why did I scape the fury of the French,
And vpde not vp the temper of their swords :
Shamelesse my life, and shamefully it ends,
Scornd by my foes, disdained of my friends.

              Bastard,

Baſtard Forgiue the world and all your earthly foes,
And call on Chriſt, who is your lateſt friend.

Iohn My tongue doth falter: *Philip*, I tell thee man,
Since *Iohn* did yeeld vnto the Prieſt of *Rome*,
Nor he nor his haue proſpred on the earth :
Curſt are his bleſſings, and his curſe is bliſſe.
But in the ſpirit I cry vnto my God,
As did the Kingly Prophet *Dauid* cry,
(Whoſe hands, as mine, with murder were attaint)
I am not he ſhall buyld the Lord a houſe,
Or rowte theſe Locuſts from the face of earth :
But if my dying heart deceaue me not,
From out theſe loynes ſhall ſpring a Kingly braunch
Whoſe armes ſhall reach vnto the gates of *Rome*,
And with his feete treads downe the Strumpets pryde,
That ſits vpon the chaire of *Babylon*.
Philip, my heart ſtrings breake, the poyſons flame
Hath ouercome in me weake Natures power,
And in the faith of Ieſu *Iohn* doth dye.

Baſtard Sée how he ſtriues for life, vnhappy Lord,
Whoſe bowells are deuided in themſelues.
This is the fruite of Poperie, when true Kings
Are ſlaine and ſhouldred out by Monkes and Friers.

Enter a Meſſenger.

Meſſ. Pleaſe it your Grace, the Barons of the Land,
Which all this while bare armes againſt the King,
Conducted by the Legate of the Pope,
Together with the Prince his Highnes Sonne,
Doo craue to be admitted to the preſence of the King.
Baſtard Your Sonne my Lord, yong *Henry* craues to ſée.
Your Maieſtie, and brings with him beſide
The Barons that reuolted from your Grace.
O piercing ſight, he fumbleth in the mouth,
His ſpeech doth faile : lift vp your ſelfe my Lord,

And

92

96

100

104

108

112

116

120

124

Raigne

And ſee the Prince to comfort you in death.

Enter *Pandulph,* yong *Henry,* the Barons with daggers
in their hands.

Prince O let me ſee my Father err he dye :
O Unckle were you here, and ſufferd him
To be thus poyſned by a damned Monke.
Ah he is dead, Father ſweete Father ſpeake.
Baſtard His ſpeach doth faile, he haſteth to his end.
Pandulph Lords, giue me leaue to ioy the dying King,
With ſight of theſe his Nobles kneeling here
With daggers in their hands, who offer vp
Their liues for ranſome of their fowle offence.
Then good my Lord, if you forgiue them all,
Lift vp your hand in token you forgiue.
Salisbury We humbly thanke your royall Maieſtie,
And vow to fight for *England* and her King :
And in the ſight of *Iohn* our ſoueraigne Lord,
In ſpight of *Lewes* and the power of *Fraunce*
Who hetherward are marching in all haſt,
We crowne yong *Henry* in his Fathers ſted.
Henry Help, help, he dyes, a Father, looke on me.
Legat K. *Iohn* farewell : in token of thy faith,
And ſigne thou dyeſt the ſeruant of the Lord,
Lift vp thy hand, that we may witnes here
Thou dyedſt the ſeruant of our Sauiour Chriſt.
Now ioy betide thy ſoule : what noyſe is this :

Enter a Meſſenger.

Meſſ. Help Lords, the Dolphin maketh hetherward
With Enſignes of deſtance in the winde,
And all our armie ſtandeth at a gaze
Expecting what their Leaders will commaund.
Baſtard Lets arme our ſelues in yong K. *Henries* right,

And

of King Iohn.

And beate the power of *Fraunce* to sea againe.
   Legat *Philip* not so, but I will to the Prince,
And bring him face to face to parle with you.
   Bastard Lord *Salsbury*, your selfe shall march with me,
So shall we bring these troubles to an ende.
   King Sweete Unckle, if thou loue thy Soueraigne,
Let not a stone of *Swinsted Abbey* stand,
But pull the house about the Friers eares :
For they haue kilde my Father and my King. Exeunt.

A parle sounded, *Lewes, Pandulph, Salsbury, &c.*

   Pandulph *Lewes* of *Fraunce*, yong *Henry Englands* King
Requires to know the reason of the claime
That thou canst make to any thing of his.
King *Iohn* that did offend is dead and gone,
See where his breathles trunke in presence lyes,
And he as heire apparant to the crowne
Is now succeeded in his Fathers roome.
   Henry Lewes, what law of Armes doth lead thee thus,
To keepe possession of my lawfull right :
Answere in fine if thou wilt take a peace,
And make surrender of my right againe,
Or trie thy title with the dint of sword ?
I tell thee Dolphin, *Henry* feares thee not,
For now the Barons cleaue vnto their King,
And what thou hast in *England* they did get.
   Lewes *Henry* of *England*, now that *Iohn* is dead
That was the chiefest enemie to *Fraunce*,
I may the rather be induced to peace.
But *Salsbury*, and you Barons of the Realme,
This strange reuolt agrees not with the oath.
That you on *Bury* Altare lately sware.
   Salsbury Nor did the oath your Highnes there did take
Agree with honour of the Prince of *Fraunce*.
   Bastard My Lord, what answere make you to the King..
                                        Dolphin

The troublesome Raigne

(not in K. John

Dolphin Faith *Philip* this I say: It bootes not me,
Nor any Prince, nor power of Christendome
To seeke to win this Iland *Albion,*
Unles he haue a partie in the Realme
By treason for to help him in his warres.
The Péeres which were the partie on my side,
Are fled from me: then bootes not me to fight,
But on conditions, as mine honour wills,
I am contented to depart the Realme.
   Henry On what conditions will your Highnes yeeld?
   Lewes That shall we thinke vpon by more aduice.
   Bastard Then Kings & Princes, let these broils haue end,
And at more leasure talke vpon the League.
Meane while to *Worster* let vs beare the King,
And there interre his bodie, as beseemes.
But first, in sight of *Lewes* heire of *Fraunce,*
Lords take the crowne, and set it on his head,
That by succession is our lawfull King.

They crowne yong Henry.

Thus *Englands* peace begins in *Henryes* Raigne,
And bloody warres are closde with happie league.
Let *England* liue but true within it selfe,
And all the world can neuer wrong her State.
Lewes, thou shalt be brauely shipt to *France,*
For neuer Frenchman got of English ground
The twentieh part that thou hast conquered.
Dolphin thy hand, to *Worster* we will march,
Lords all lay hands to beare your Soueraigne
With obsequies of honor to his graue:
If *Englands* Péeres and people ioyne in one,
Nor Pope, nor *Fraunce,* nor *Spaine* can doo them wrong.

F I N I S.